In Want of a Wife

Pemberley House, Book One

NOELLE ADAMS

Pemberley House

IN WANT OF A WIFE
IF I LOVED YOU LESS
LOVED NONE BUT YOU

ONE

Liz Berkley woke up at five on a Thursday morning so that she could be first in line at an estate sale, but someone had beaten her to it.

Her first clue was the shiny gray SUV already parked on the grass beside the long driveway. After pulling her own small, inexpensive sedan beside it, she encountered her second clue—the figure of a man on the front porch near the door.

She scowled.

She'd gotten up before dawn to be first in line. She'd been going to estate sales for her family's antiques business for seven years now—ever since she'd been eighteen years old. She knew that arriving at a sale of this size and quality at six in the morning always allowed her to be first in line.

What the hell was that man doing here?

He better not be trying for her Brandt paintings.

Since the oil paintings were the only items of real value at this sale—at least as far as could be discerned from the listing—it was likely that he *was* after the paintings.

And he'd gotten here first.

The man didn't turn around as she approached the house. He made no sign that he'd even heard her. He was staring down at his phone, tapping out a message. He was significantly overdressed for an estate sale. Well-tailored trousers and an Oxford in a small gray-and-white-checked fabric. It was tucked in perfectly and unwrinkled, despite the early hour. His clothes and shoes and car were obviously expensive.

She scowled again at his back.

She'd barely formed the expression when he turned around, and she had to do some quick rearrangement of her facial muscles. "Good morning!" she said brightly, giving him a smile that was as sincere as she could muster.

It wasn't his fault that she had an overly competitive nature and a constant, low-level anxiety about the financial struggles of her family's business. She'd still be in the first group of numbers to be admitted into the house. The company handling this sale was solid, but they always priced original paintings too low, so this was her best chance of getting her hands on Brandt paintings at a price low enough for successful resale. She could get to the paintings before him. She wasn't going to hold it against him that he'd somehow arrived first.

The man's eyes made a quick route from her face and down her body. She was dressed casually in jean capris and a cute top and cardigan. He wouldn't be able to tell that every piece she wore had been bought on clearance. She couldn't tell from his expression whether he liked how she looked.

"Good morning," he said. He didn't return her smile.

Fighting a prickle of annoyance at his unfriendly expression, she kept her voice cheerful. "You got out here early."

"So did you."

With the same sober expression, the man scrawled a number on the top sheet of a pad of sticky notes and handed the note to her.

Two.

She was Number Two.

She was used to being Number One.

The man clearly knew what he was doing since he'd brought the pad of sticky notes. She had one in her small purse since she was normally the one to pass out street numbers.

"I haven't seen you around before," she said, trying once again to be friendly. Since they were going to be standing here for a couple of hours, they might as well chat.

"No."

Her attempt not to scowl again—right in his face—made her jaw sore. A normal person would have added a little more to the conversation, given her something to respond to.

She wanted to know who this guy was and what he was doing here.

He appeared to be in his late twenties or early thirties. He had steel-gray eyes, high cheekbones, and a strong chiseled jaw. He was about five inches taller than Liz's five seven, and he had a straight posture and a very fine pair of shoulders.

He was one of the best-looking men she had ever seen.

That recognition and the bone-deep attraction that came with it vied with exasperation in her mind. It wasn't clear which would predominate.

She waited, but he didn't say anything else. Annoyance was quickly subsuming her visceral appreciation of his appearance.

"I'm Liz," she said with a smile, holding her hand out to him. She was going to make him follow the basics of civility whether he wanted to or not.

He slowly reached out and shook her hand, his eyes observing her with a quiet scrutiny she didn't understand. His hand was big and warm.

Her eyes widened as she waited several seconds and wondered if he was actually refusing to return the introduction.

Then finally he said, "Vince," just before he dropped his hand.

Vince.

She was hit by another wave of attraction as his eyes held hers. The man was way too good-looking. It wasn't entirely fair. That kind of sexiness could be a weapon when left in the wrong hands.

"Do you go to estate sales a lot?" she asked, trying to think of a natural topic of conversation instead of standing there drooling over him.

"Not if I can help it." His tone was dry. Just shy of bitter.

"If you don't like them, why get up so early to come to this one?"

The question was perhaps a little pushy, but it was still well within the bounds of politeness. She really wanted an answer because this man was a frustrating enigma.

He responded only with a one-shouldered shrug.

Her lip curled up before she could stop it, and she looked down at the sticky note in her hand to hide the expression. Could Vince be any less friendly?

She was a nice, outgoing person. Other people usually liked her and talked to her easily. And yet trying to make conversation with this man was like pulling teeth—painful and achingly slow.

The NUMBER TWO written on the sticky note taunted her.

She couldn't believe he'd beat her out here this morning. Her sister, Jane, always told her she was too competitive for her own good. That life wasn't a race. That living like it was would only lead to needless frustration.

She knew Jane was right, and she did (at times) try to work on it. Relax. Let go of her tight hold on the world. Mind her own business and let the universe do what it wanted. Gripping it so tightly wouldn't necessarily keep it from falling apart.

But the knowledge that a man as rude as Vince had beaten her this morning grated on her anyway. As she stared down at the scrawled number, she mentally planned her attack once she entered the house. She'd been to many estate sales organized by this company, so she knew how this one would be handled. At seven, someone from the company would arrive to take over the numbers, so she could leave the line then—go back to her car or walk around. At exactly eight, the first ten numbers would be allowed into the house as the first group. Vince would go in first, but she'd studied the layout of the house. She could get around him in the entryway and go straight to the dining room where one of the Brandt paintings was hanging on the wall.

The paintings were small, so she could just pick it up instead of waiting for a staff member to mark it as sold. Then she'd head straight up the stairs to the master bedroom where the other painting was located.

She could get to both of them while everyone else was milling around getting their bearings.

Vince might have gotten here first, but he wasn't going to get her paintings. They were done by Felix Brandt, a well-known local artist, and they were a rare find. They might

5

look like normal landscapes, but their popularity was increasing, and Brandt had stopped painting about twenty years ago. He didn't have long left to live. As mercenary as it sounded, his death would at least double the value of the paintings.

Berkley's Antiques had been existing on the verge of bankruptcy for years now. Her family *needed* those paintings.

She just had to beat Vince to them.

When she looked up at him, he was watching her again, and there was a slight glint in the charcoal gray of his eyes.

Like he knew how she was feeling. Like it amused him that he'd won the first round of their unspoken competition.

She stewed inwardly while she gave him an overly sweet smile with a challenge just under the surface—the one her friend Em always called her Blair Waldorf smile.

Vince could laugh now.

But he wasn't going to get her paintings.

Two hours later, Liz had to push through a crowd of about thirty people so she could get back to the front to be let in with the first group. While she'd been waiting at the door, she'd mostly played on her phone since Vince was obviously not going to be friendly. When the staff member from the liquidation company had arrived, she'd gone to walk around the yard and stretch her legs and then sit in her car to talk to Jane on the phone.

It was almost eight now. They'd be let into the house soon.

She had her plan of attack plotted and replotted in her mind.

She was ready.

She gave a cheerful greeting to Chad, who was handing out numbers and manning the door. She knew him from many estate sales in the past. She showed him her sticky note with the number two written on it and took her place behind Vince, who was idly scrolling through something on his phone.

As if he didn't have a care in the world.

As if it didn't matter to him whether he acquired the Brandt paintings or anything else.

It mattered to Liz.

This was her job. She'd worked with her father all through college, and then after she'd graduated four years ago, she'd taken on a lot of the buying for her family's large antiques business in Abingdon, Virginia. She loved going to flea markets and searching out treasures. She also loved attending auctions and strategizing to get the best price on the most valuable items.

Estate sales were different, but she was good at them too.

Her grandfather had opened Berkley's Antiques sixty-five years ago, and the store had been a success and supported his family for decades. When her father took over at her grandfather's death, things should have continued in the same manner since antiques were thriving in this area.

But her father had married her mother. Liz's mother had a good heart, but she had no head for business and was a profligate spender. She'd decided she wanted to "help" with the business, and she'd almost run it into the ground.

It was only two years ago that her father had admitted to Liz how dangerously close to bankruptcy they were. They'd even explored the possibility of a merger with Darcy's, the most successful of their rivals in the Abingdon antiques market. But Darcy's had refused to let them keep their own name on the store—even though the Berkley name had been established for sixty-five years and the Darcy name only ten. Her parents refused to sign a contract that would remove the Berkley name, no matter how the deal would have saved them financially.

So Liz was constantly scrambling to acquire pieces that would turn a good profit so she could help dig her family out of the hole. And Jane had spent months of work and effort in improving the store's website and adding online listings on eBay, Etsy, and Amazon Marketplace. Now more than half their purchases were online. Between Jane and Liz, they'd managed to salvage the business, but it was still always teetering on the brink.

Liz couldn't relax. There was too much at stake.

This was more than a job to her. It was her duty. Her family.

And Vince beating her here this morning wasn't going to keep her from what she needed to do.

He didn't put down his phone until the very last moment, right as Chad was opening the door to admit the first ten people into the house.

The entryway was wide, so Liz tried to get around Vince to head to the dining room, but she quickly realized that he was moving in that direction too. His long legs made fast strides down the hall.

He was walking, but she had to speed up to a run to reach his side as they entered the dining room.

That room was almost entirely filled with a huge dining table and ten big chairs—made to look impressive but only knockoffs that weren't worth very much. Since there was so little walking space left in the room, Liz was able to block Vince's access to the most direct route to the painting. He had to go around to the other side of the table to reach the Brandt, which was hanging on the wall above a brick fireplace.

Liz moved fast, but Vince's legs were a lot longer than hers. As soon as he accelerated to a run, she knew he was going to beat her, despite having a slightly longer distance to cover.

He did beat her.

He got to the painting she wanted first.

Their eyes met across the few feet of distance. Both of them were breathing heavily. Liz was hot and frustrated and angry and ridiculously attracted to him.

And he was gloating. *Gloating.*

Not smiling. He never did that. But that glint appeared in his eyes again, the one that proved he was pleased he'd come out ahead.

As if this was a game to him and not her family's well-being.

All this took place within a couple of seconds, but Liz was nothing if not a fast thinker.

As soon as Vince's hand closed down around the carved frame of the painting, she turned on her heel and started moving out of the room.

If he was going to get this painting, she was going to get the other one.

He was obviously faster than her, but he was slowed down by summoning a staff member over to the first painting so it would be marked as sold.

There was someone in the room, so it didn't take long, but it gave Liz a decent head start.

She would have easily gotten to the other Brandt upstairs well before Vince had she not been delayed by an elderly couple making their way up the stairs side by side.

Liz couldn't get around them, and she was far too nice a person to just push through between them even if it meant Vince would catch up.

He did catch up.

He was right on her heels when the couple finally made it to the second floor.

In the moment before she took the last step up, Liz saw Farrah, a middle-aged woman who worked for the liquidation company, loitering in the hallway. Liz had known Farrah since she was a little girl and had attended estate sales with her father.

She caught Farrah's eye and inclined her head slightly toward Vince behind her.

Farrah knew what she meant.

When Liz was clear of the older couple, she took off at a dead run toward the master bedroom. Vince was right beside her, and in normal circumstances he'd have outpaced her. But Farrah casually moved directly into his path, nearly causing a collision.

"Oh no!" Farrah said in a voice that sounded genuinely apologetic. "I'm so sorry! Let me get out of your way."

Despite being slowed down by Farrah's interference, Vince almost overtook Liz again, but the delay was just long enough for her to reach the painting a few moments before him.

She grabbed the frame, panting and grinning victoriously. "Mine!"

Vince was breathing fast too, and his face was slightly flushed. His eyes narrowed. "You cheated."

Liz could barely hold back a rush of giggles, but she managed to widen her eyes and maintain an innocent expression. "Were there rules I didn't know about?"

Vince gave her another glare and backed away as Farrah came up grinning to mark the painting as sold.

He didn't stick around to argue. Just gave her one last look before he turned and left the room.

"Where did *he* come from?" Farrah asked in a hushed voice.

"I have no idea. He obviously knows what the Brandts are worth, but I've never seen the man before. He got the other painting, but at least I snagged this one. I think this is the better one anyway."

"You should check out the closet in the guest bedroom. Looks like some good stuff there."

Liz nodded. "That's where I'm headed now. The listing mentioned vintage clothes and handbags."

In the closet, Liz immediately found a Louis Vuitton handbag from the seventies that was ridiculously underpriced. She grabbed it excitedly and gave the shoes a cursory glance, quickly recognizing there was nothing of value. Then she started to search the clothes.

She found two vintage dresses in good condition, so she added them to her pile. She'd reached the back of the closet when she saw something hanging in a garment bag. She pulled it out and stepped out of the closet so she'd have enough room to unzip it.

Inside was a wedding dress.

A beautiful vintage wedding dress with a lace bodice and a gracefully flowing silk skirt. The style was simple, but the craftsmanship was top of the line, and the embroidery on the bodice was intricate and delicate.

Liz stared at the dress with a craving that was physical. Visceral.

She wanted it the way she wanted chocolate.

She checked for tags, but there was no evidence of a designer. Then she inspected some of the seams and realized it had been made by hand. The seamstress was brilliant. The fabric wasn't yellowing so had been well cared for. The dress had to be at least fifty years old.

"Are you taking that?" The male voice came from behind her.

Liz jumped and reddened like she'd been caught doing something intimate. She turned to see Vince coming into the room. He was carrying a small antique clock.

She'd been planning to check out that clock if it was still available, so it was slightly annoying that he had his hands on it. The clock wasn't as good as her own finds, however.

"Yes. I'm taking it."

Now that she'd touched the wedding dress, she was quite sure she'd never be able to let it go.

She wasn't even sure she'd be able to hand it over to her father to sell.

She might have to buy it for herself.

Her friend had a wedding dress she kept hanging in an empty bedroom—even though Em was never planning to get married. She'd bought it just for herself. If Em could have a wedding dress without any sign of a marriage in the future, why couldn't Liz?

"Those are mine too." She nodded toward the two dresses draped over the Louis Vuitton handbag.

Vince nodded, looking unconcerned. He didn't appear to recognize the value of the items she'd chosen, so she figured he wasn't well informed on vintage fashion. He might know which paintings to go after first, but he wasn't as good at this as she was.

He gave the room a cursory inspection. Ran his hand over the garments hanging in the closet. Then headed to the door.

He definitely wasn't here to look at clothes.

He paused before he stepped out. "Is that worth a lot?" He nodded toward the wedding dress, looking genuinely curious.

Because his interest seemed sincere, she answered him without any tartness. "Maybe. But its value is a lot more than monetary. A woman made this—either for herself or for a member of her family. She sewed her life into this dress— all her hopes and dreams and love and feelings. It's... priceless."

When she finished, she was a little embarrassed by the earnestness of her answer. She was known for having a quick wit and a sharp tongue. For always being ready for a debate. Not for sentimentality.

She was even more self-conscious when she glanced over at Vince and saw he was staring at her soberly, without even a hint of a smile.

She couldn't read his expression. At all.

She cleared her throat. "Anyway, I'm not surprised that clothes don't hold any interest to you, but this might be a better find than either of the paintings. Someone really slipped up in not recognizing the quality of this."

"Ah."

That was all he said. *Ah.*

She scowled again at his back as he walked out the door.

~

For the rest of the day, Vince Darcy couldn't stop thinking about Liz.

It was annoying.

She was merely a random woman. One who had gotten in his way—since he'd told his mother he'd come back with both Brandt paintings—but one who shouldn't linger in his thoughts this way.

But she was there on his drive back to Abingdon, prickling in his mind like an unanswered question or a word he couldn't quite recall. And she was still there when he worked for a few hours in the office of Darcy's, the antiques store his parents had opened ten years ago. Each time he paused from cleaning up last year's accounting so they'd be ready for this year's taxes, he would picture a pair of vivid green eyes, their expression shifting seamlessly between laughter and challenge.

It wasn't like Liz was drop-dead beautiful or anything. Her eyes and mouth were too big, and both her small nose and her chin had a slight upward tilt, making her features interesting more than classic. Her hair was gorgeous—thick and wavy and brown, even pulled into a ponytail the way it had been this morning. And her body was fit and curvy and...

14

Well, it was good. He visualized her ass and her breasts as much as he did her eyes, and his body definitely appreciated the mental image.

But still.

She wasn't gorgeous, and this morning had been a meaningless encounter.

He shouldn't still be thinking about her. He'd always liked women. He dated often, and he appreciated them on all levels. Not just physically. But he couldn't remember being as leveled by a woman as he was by Liz this morning.

It was annoying.

She was annoying.

The whole situation was annoying.

And he was still vaguely annoyed by it when his mother arrived in the shop at two in the afternoon.

She and his father had had a successful dental practice in Richmond for twenty-five years before they'd retired early. They'd opened a small antiques shop in Abingdon since they'd both been avid antiquers and had been too young to not do anything in their retirement. Abingdon already had a lot of antiques stores since the town had a solid tourist industry and a quaint historical downtown area. They'd never expected their little shop to take off the way it had, but four years ago they'd had to expand into a much larger space on Main Street.

Right now their only real competition was Berkley's Antiques, and that one had been established sixty-five years ago and was evidently not doing as well financially as it should be because the family was always trying to do a deal with Darcy's.

According to Riot, the silly, ridiculously named young woman who worked the cash register at his parents' store, the

Berkleys still resented the fact that the Darcys had insisted on keeping their own name on their store.

Riot would know. She was one of the Berkley daughters and had taken the job at the Darcy store to spite her parents.

The whole thing felt rather adolescent to him. He didn't like artificial drama, and he didn't particularly like Riot and wasn't sure why his parents had even hired her.

But he'd only moved back to town and started helping out with the business a few weeks ago, so he wasn't in a position to question decisions that had been made before he got here.

His first priority was cleaning up these accounts.

They were a mess, and he was amazed the IRS hadn't come after his parents already since the financial side of the business had been handled in a rather slapdash way. Vince had majored in business with an emphasis in finance and then gotten an MBA. He'd had a good job in the finance department of a growing company in Blacksburg with an international reach, but then his father had died three months ago.

His mother hadn't wanted to give up the store, but there was no way she could handle it on her own. His brother Robert was an officer in the Navy and didn't know anything about business. That left Vince.

He'd suggested she might want to reconsider the Berkley's offer since that would have taken a lot of the responsibility off her, but she hadn't wanted to give up what she'd built with her husband in his last years. If he'd pushed, Vince probably could have convinced her. But she'd just lost her husband, and he couldn't bring himself to take this away from her too.

So he'd quit his job and moved to Abingdon for his mother.

It wouldn't have been his first choice. Or his tenth choice. But it wouldn't be forever, and it was what he needed to do right now.

"This is gorgeous," his mother said, leaning over the Brandt landscape he'd bought at the estate sale that morning. "I'm so glad you were able to get it."

"I'm sorry I couldn't get the other one."

"It's okay."

"It's not okay. I almost had it. I would have had it... had other people played fair." His voice was dry at the end, mostly because he was hit again with a vision of Liz's laughing eyes, the quiver of victory at the corners of her lush mouth as she met his eyes after claiming the second painting.

His mother laughed. She was small and slim and always slightly messy, with wrinkles in her dress and flyaways in her gray-brown hair. She was one of the smartest people Vince had ever known, but practicality wasn't one of her gifts. "You'll have to get used to those estate sales. They're sometimes supercompetitive. I've seen knock-down, drag-out fights over items before. Once, I saw two guys fighting over an antique set of toy soldiers—still in the original packaging—and the company had to call the police!"

Vince chuckled at that. "It wasn't that bad this morning, but I still should have gotten the second painting. She somehow got a staff member to run interference for her, so she reached it before I did."

"Who was she?" There was the slightest glint in his mother's gray eyes that should have set off warning bells in his mind.

"I don't know. But she'd obviously been to a bunch of these sales before since everyone knew her. She looked to

17

be in her midtwenties. Brunette. Big green eyes. Kind of annoying."

The glint in his mom's eyes intensified. One corner of her mouth twitched up. "You noticed her."

He knew what his mom was thinking and was hit with a wave of defensiveness. "Of course I noticed her. She was racing me for those paintings and then cheated to get one of them."

"I see."

"Don't act like that. She was just some woman."

"I know who she is."

Despite his attempt to remain casual, he straightened up at that. "Do you? She said her name was Liz."

"It is." With another amused twitch of a smile, his mother added, "Do you want to know who she is?"

Of course he wanted to know who she was.

He wanted to know everything about her.

He managed to keep his expression bland as he said, "You obviously want to tell, so you might as well."

"She's one of Riot's sisters."

"What?" That surprised him so much he couldn't hide his emotional investment in the conversation. "You can't be serious."

"I am. The Berkleys have three daughters. She's the middle one. Riot is the youngest."

"I can't believe that. She was annoying, but she seemed smart and competent. Riot is—" He cut off the words since he didn't want to be mean or offend his mother, who had hired Riot and appeared to like her.

"Riot is immature. Yes, I know that. But she's not as brainless as she acts. And I think Liz is the smartest of the three."

"So she works for Berkleys?"

"Yes."

"Great. That's just great."

Just his luck. The frustrating woman he couldn't get out of his mind was also their store's main competition in town.

He briefly wondered if she'd known who he was and whether that had caused her obvious rivalry, but he quickly dismissed that possibility. She hadn't known he was a Darcy. She probably would have acted the same with anyone who had challenged her for those paintings.

It would be her nature to never back down.

"She obviously made an impression on you."

"Not that much of an impression. It just bothers me I couldn't get both paintings for you."

"I told you. Don't worry about that. Your dad always said the store was doing just fine, and most of our big commissions come from private deals anyway. But it looks like Liz riled you up, and I haven't seen a woman rile you up that way in... well, ever maybe."

"She didn't rile me up," he lied.

Rile was exactly what she'd done to him.

"Uh-huh. I'm just saying. I don't know her personally, but everyone in town seems to love her. It wouldn't be a bad idea for you to start thinking about getting serious about a woman."

"Please, Mom."

"Don't give me that tone. You're twenty-nine. Next year you'll be thirty. And as far as I can tell, you're always dating someone, but it's never serious."

"I just haven't found the right woman yet."

"That could very well be true. But even if the right woman shows up, it won't matter if you're afraid to commit to her."

"I'm not afraid to—"

His mom rolled her eyes. "Okay. I'll rephrase. It won't matter if you *refuse* to commit to her."

"I'll commit when I find the right woman."

"That's an excuse."

He didn't like this kind of conversation. It made him feel awkward and vulnerable. He had to struggle not to snap at his mother. "Maybe. But it feels like the truth to me."

"Okay. I just want you to be happy, and I think you'll be happier with a wife."

"I don't need a wife."

"I know you don't *need* one. But you seem like you've been skating through life, living only on the surface. You'll be happier if you'll let yourself love someone. Take care of someone. Go deep."

He felt more vulnerable than ever, partly because a small part of him knew his mother was speaking the truth. Things had come easy for him most of his life since he had the kind of intelligence that solved problems quickly, and he had a naturally professional appearance that other people respected and admired. He'd done well in his career. He'd had a nice apartment in Blacksburg and a social group that allowed him to date a lot without trying too hard. But he hadn't cultivated close friendships or real intimacy with women. Something had always held him back.

His mother added, "You've been this way ever since Georgie died."

His heart clamped down at his sister's name. She'd been three years younger than him and had been a freshman at UVA when he was a senior.

She'd been sweet and warmhearted and intoxicated with life—and the attention she'd started getting from men. His parents had asked him to take care of her, and he'd tried.

He'd tried.

But she'd hooked up with a loser boyfriend, and one night he'd driven her back to the dorms when both of them were drunk. He'd run the car off the road. It had rolled down a steep embankment.

Both Georgie and the boyfriend had died.

Vince knew it wasn't his fault. He didn't blame himself.

But the knowledge of his failure remained like a knot in his gut. He hadn't tried very hard—at anything but work— ever since.

He hadn't gone deep.

He had the sudden, inexplicable image of that wedding dress Liz had been holding this morning. Then he saw her wearing it, walking down the aisle toward a waiting groom.

His heart jumped with something like excitement, and he immediately pushed the ridiculous picture out of his head. He was clearly letting his mother's sentimentality affect his logic.

He said, "I can go deep without getting married."

"Of course you can. If that's what you want, I'll be very happy for you. Just don't keep skating on the surface of life. It's so much more rewarding if you're willing to invest. Go deep."

He sat and stared blankly at his computer screen, fighting conflicting waves of defensiveness, embarrassment, and something like guilt.

Since he wasn't looking at his mother, he was surprised when she was suddenly standing right beside him. She reached down to pat his cheek. "I'm not disappointed in you, Vince."

He cleared his throat. "I know."

"Do you? I'm so proud of you. I can't tell you how much it means to me that you've moved here to help me out with the store. I know what you had to give up."

He shifted uncomfortably in his chair. "I didn't give up that much."

"Yes, you did. You gave up the life you'd made for yourself and your independence. I wish you didn't have to do it."

"I don't mind. I wanted to help."

"I know. You always try to take care of people. You were a good brother to Georgie. What happened to her can't control the rest of your life."

"It doesn't."

"Are you sure? Because I'm not. It changed you— even more than it changed the rest of us." Resistance was rising inside Vince at his mother's words, and she must have been able to see it on his face. Because she altered her tone as she added, "Anyway, the least I can do to make sure you're happy is insist you move out of the house this weekend."

"I told you I'm fine living with you for a while, if you need me to."

"I know you said that. But you're a grown man, and you shouldn't have to live with your old mom. I'm really fine. I can navigate the house now without weeping over everything that reminds me of your dad. You're doing enough by moving here and helping with the business. You don't have to live with me too. So move into Pemberley House with Charlie. It's time."

Despite his assurances to his mother, he was relieved at her pressure. He was willing to do what he needed to help his mother, but he'd be much more comfortable if he could once again have his own place. "Okay. I will."

"I know you loved your old apartment, but Pemberley House is something special. I'm so glad Charlie's family has a unit there and he was looking for a roommate. You're going to love it."

"I'm sure I will."

"Your dad and I looked at buying a unit there when they went on the market, but we decided we'd be happier in a house. But the building and estate are gorgeous. And I don't think it's all old people living there either."

"Uh-huh." Pemberley House was a historic mansion on a large piece of property in Abingdon that had been converted into condos ten years ago. His friend Charlie's parents had bought a unit as soon as they'd come onto the market, planning to use it when they retired, but Charlie had recently gone through a painful breakup with his girlfriend of five years, and he'd needed a new place to live. Since the condo was sitting empty, his parents had offered it to him.

Vince was happy to share the place with Charlie for a while, but he could well imagine the other tenants of the building. The prices were too high for most young people. Nearly all the homeowners were retired couples and middle-aged professionals.

"There *are* some young people there." His mother slanted him a mischievous smile. "Your little friend lives there."

"My little friend?" He really had no idea who she was talking about.

"Liz Berkley."

He gave a jerk. "She lives there?"

"Yes. Her family owns a unit. She's living in it with her older sister right now. So you should have plenty of opportunity to get to know her."

"Oh."

He told himself that wasn't an important piece of information. Liz held no particular interest to him, other than being vaguely annoying.

But his body didn't seem to understand that fact. His blood was pumping with excitement.

His heart didn't understand it either.

It was beating way too fast.

TWO

Liz had spent her twenty-five years surrounded by beautiful things, so there was no reason for her to be so consumed by the lingering memory of Vince's handsome face and fine body.

She couldn't get him out of her mind.

Those broad shoulders. Big hands. Wry gray eyes. Mobile mouth.

She kept seeing them for the rest of the day, and every time she visualized him, she got excited all over again.

She would have gotten over it quickly. She was sure of it. She wasn't the kind of woman who acted this way about men, even very handsome and incredibly sexy ones. But she wasn't given the chance to forget about Vince.

She nearly collided with him on Thursday evening, stepping onto the elevator in her own building.

Pemberley House had been built in 1895 by a millionaire named Edward Knightley, who wanted to indulge his new wife. The original mansion had twenty-five bedrooms, a grand ballroom, and fifty acres of gardens surrounded by a stone wall. The property was passed down through each generation of the Knightleys, despite the fact that its upkeep ended up bankrupting the family. Finally, ten years ago, its current owner gave up at last and converted the mansion into twelve different condo units, each one unique and beautiful and quickly snapped up by local families, including Liz's own.

She and her older sister, Jane, lived in the southeast, upper-floor unit. The other residents were older couples or middle-aged professional women. The only unmarried men at Pemberley House were sixty-five-year-old Mr. Woodson and the only surviving Knightley, a thoughtful, competent man who lived in a detached cottage and managed the property.

Liz had no idea what Vince was doing here, stepping off the elevator that had been installed when the mansion was converted. But it was definitely him.

Exactly as she remembered with his steel-gray eyes, his lean, athletic body, and his sober, slightly arrogant expression.

She had her arms full of bunches of flowers since her mother had overdone the decorations at the luncheon she'd hosted earlier that day and Liz had offered to take the leftovers. She couldn't see well over the tops of the tulips and hydrangeas she carried, and she started to step onto the elevator as soon as the doors slid open since most of the residents took the stairs.

She made a little exclamation of surprise as she almost ran into the man stepping off, and then she gaped for a moment as she took in his appearance.

Vince.

Every bit as unjustly handsome as he'd been this morning.

When she'd never expected to see him again.

Her response was like the afternoon she'd found a Chippendale table for sale at a flea market for ten dollars. Exactly the same rush of excitement, thrill of unexpected delight, wave of visceral appreciation.

What was he doing here?

And why did she still find him so unbelievably attractive?

He was now dressed in jeans and a blue-gray T-shirt that was slightly damp with sweat spots, despite the fact that it was a coolish spring evening. The sweat did nothing to make him less sexy.

"I'm so sorry," Liz said when she'd recovered enough to make her voice work. "I didn't see you there."

She smiled at him, determined to be pleasant despite their rivalry that morning.

He paused and reached back to hold open the elevator doors so she could get on, but nothing close to a smile passed across his expression. He didn't reply with words either.

Rattled by her response to him and by his lack of response to her, Liz fumbled with her armful of flowers in an attempt to hit the button for her floor.

Evidently understanding what her awkward maneuverings were aimed at, Vince reached over to press the button for the second floor. Pemberley House was three floors, and the six upper units were all two stories each.

"Thank you," she said with another smile. "I didn't expect to see you here. Are you visiting someone?"

It didn't speak well of her—at all—but her initial feeling at this thought was jealousy. *Jealousy.* That Vince had been visiting Em or Anne or another of the single women who lived here.

She didn't want him dating any of her friends. Despite his obnoxious character, part of her wanted him for herself.

He made a slight gesture of his head that might have been a shake, like his answer to her question was no, but again he didn't use any words. His gray eyes were on her face as the elevator doors closed, but there was still no hint of a smile.

"What the hell?" she demanded to the empty elevator as it started to ascend.

What kind of man didn't bother to answer a direct question or not smile in response to a friendly greeting?

Definitely not a very nice one.

He might be handsome, but that was clearly all he had going for him.

This morning obviously hadn't been an aberration for him. It was his normal character.

If Em or Anne or anyone else wanted him, then they could have him.

She preferred friendly people.

When the elevator reached her floor, she hurried to the front door of her unit. She let herself in and immediately realized that her sister and friends were all out on the terrace.

Ever since she and Jane had moved in, they'd had a regular Thursday-night ritual with Em and Anne. Since Liz was later than normal today, the others had started without her.

She dropped the flowers onto the marble-topped island and then made her way out through the french doors and onto the terrace, where Jane and her two friends were gathered around the wrought iron table.

"I ran into a very rude man in the elevator," she announced as she pulled an empty chair back from the table. "He was at the estate sale this morning. He was rude then, and he's still rude now."

The others all laughed, proving they knew exactly who she was talking about.

"He hasn't said hi or smiled or anything," Em said with a shake of her pretty blond head. "Even though he's walked from the parking lot six times now and has obviously seen us sitting here."

"Six times? What's he doing?"

Em poured their favorite pink champagne into a glass and handed it to Liz. "He's moving in."

"Moving in?" Liz felt that rush of excitement again, even though most of her mind had already decided that she didn't like Vince at all. "Who's he moving in with? The only empty unit is—"

"The Fieldings." Em was a year older than Liz, but they'd been friends for most of their lives. She was the only daughter of a rich, indulgent father, and so she was used to getting her way and taking control of conversations, events, and situations. But she had the biggest heart Liz had ever known. "Their son, Charlie, is moving in. He's had a painful breakup with a long-term girlfriend, so he needs a new place to live. And evidently he's gotten himself a roommate." She paused for effect. "A Darcy roommate."

"*Darcy?*" Liz's gaze flew to Anne, who'd dated one of the Darcy sons in college. But it couldn't be this man. His name hadn't been Vince.

"Not Robert," Anne said quietly. "He's still in the Navy. This is Vince."

Liz tried not to be relieved, but she was. It was completely irrational, but she didn't want Anne to have emotional ties to Vince. He might be obnoxious, but he felt like *hers*. She didn't want him to be Anne's.

"He's the older one." Jane managed to get a few words in before Em answered again. Jane was twenty-seven and had always been prettier and more popular than Liz— with the slim build and dark, silky hair that her mother and

29

Riot also had—but the two sisters were very close and had lived together for four years now. "Em talked to his mom earlier today and got the whole scoop."

"What's the scoop?"

Em cleared her throat, taking control of the conversation again. "He's twenty-nine. He worked in the finance department for some superstar company in Blacksburg for a long time, but he's moved backed to help his mom with the store, now that his dad has died."

Liz's chest contracted strangely. "Oh. I guess that's pretty nice of him."

"Mrs. Darcy is afraid that he's only doing it out of duty. That it's not what he really wants. Maybe he's been pouting or something—I don't know. She's obviously worried about him. But she thinks it will be good for him anyway. She says he needs a wife."

Experiencing that same sudden tightening of her chest, Liz managed to keep her tone light. "If he's going to move back to help her, he should do it willingly and not be resentful about it. And I'm not sure why she thinks he's going to settle down just because she wants him to. He looks like the kind of guy who's going to do exactly what he wants."

"That's what I think too, but if he's here, she'll be able to keep her eye on him. She was even hinting that I would be a good match for him, but I had to tell her that I'm not planning to get married." Em had dated in college, but she hadn't dated since. She had plenty of money and plenty of friends and a job working for the local newspaper. It hardly paid anything, but it gave her something to do. She had thousands of followers on Instagram. She'd always claimed to be perfectly happy without a romantic partner, and as far as Liz could tell, she'd meant it. "But I'm thinking one of you might be a good match for him. I told Mrs. Darcy I'd see what I could do."

Liz met Jane's eyes with a smiling shake of her head and then turned to Anne, who was the quietest of the four of them, exchanging with her a similarly amused glance.

Best to make light of it, rather than let herself feel what she'd first felt at the idea. Resistance. She didn't want Vince to be paired up with anyone else.

But she also didn't want any of her friends or sisters to know that she'd had such a strong reaction to the man. She'd be teased to no end, and then they'd probably embarrass her in trying to get them together.

She could just picture Vince's cool, lofty glare at her friends' indiscreet matchmaking attempts.

She wasn't going to let that happen.

"It might be weird for Anne," Em pronounced in her normal confident tone, "since she dated his brother. He'll do for Jane or Liz though. And just think, if you married a Darcy, then maybe your families could go through with the merger of the two companies and you wouldn't always be worried about money."

"Not worrying about money would be nice, but that guy is too cool and intimidating for me," Jane said. She'd always dated warm, friendly men who were able to draw out her reserved sweetness.

"And I could never go for a guy who doesn't smile," Liz added. "So he's yours."

"I don't want him." Em swallowed down the last of the champagne in her glass with a frown.

"Then he won't work for any of us. His mom is out of luck." Despite the detachment in her voice, Liz's eyes followed the tall, upright figure as it strode quickly from the

31

parking area to the building, carrying two boxes stacked on top of each other.

"Maybe he's just shy or something. Maybe he's not as rude as he seems." Then, as if to test her theory, Em stood up and leaned over the railing to call down, "Are you moving everything in today?"

Liz leaned over to see that Vince had stopped on the sidewalk to look up to their terrace. For just a moment his gaze met hers over the distance but then shifted almost immediately to Em.

Liz wondered whether he'd speak, now that he'd been confronted by a direct question. Surely even he wouldn't be quite so impolite as to ignore it.

"Yes," he said curtly, starting to walk again.

"There's already furniture in the unit," Em said, sitting back down with a satisfied smile. "So I guess he and the Fielding son are just going to use what's already in there."

"Oh look," Jane said, before anyone could reply to Em's last comment. "Here's someone else. Maybe this is the Fielding. You said his name is Charlie?"

"Yes. That must be him."

The second man looked about the same age as Vince, but he had lighter hair and wasn't as tall. He was carrying a large box.

Em was never one to let her questions go unanswered. She stood up again and called down when the man approached. "Good evening."

The man stopped and looked up with a smile. "Hello there!"

"He sounds a lot friendlier," Jane said softly, standing up and moving to Em's side to look down.

"Are you moving in too?" Em asked.

"Yes. My parents own one of the upper units, so they're letting me use it."

"Excellent. We're glad to have you in the building. When you're done moving in, stop by to say hi. And bring Vince with you. We're hanging out right next door."

"I will," the man said with another wide smile.

When he'd disappeared into the building, Liz waited until Jane and Em sat down before she said, "Well, at least one of our new neighbors is a nice guy."

"Give Vince a chance. Maybe he's not so bad." That was Jane, who had always been much nicer than Liz.

"Okay," Liz replied. "I'll withhold my judgment until I have a real conversation with him, but I don't hold out much hope for his being a nice guy, after what I witnessed this morning and just now."

"I think he's a match for one of you," Em said. "I've got a feeling about it, and you know how good my feelings always are."

The others laughed, and Liz didn't bother trying to argue.

But she already suspected that Vince wasn't a nice guy, and it didn't matter how sexy he was.

He wasn't a match for her.

~

An hour later, they were still chatting on the terrace when there was a knock on the door.

The reaction was immediate and kind of amusing. They all jumped up and ran inside excitedly.

Since she was one of the people who lived in this unit, Liz beat Em to answering the knock. She swung the door open to see Vince's handsome glower.

Beside him, the other man was smiling, so Liz smiled back at him. "Come on in. I'm glad you came over."

It was clear in the first two minutes that Vince had been dragged over here against his wishes. He didn't speak and didn't smile. Just sat stiffly in the chair Liz gestured him into. His friend Charlie was a third-grade teacher, and his family obviously had a lot of money.

Charlie loved the historic mansion and loved the well-kept grounds and loved his room in the unit next door and basically loved everything about his new living situation. He certainly seemed to enjoy having an audience of four friendly, attractive young women.

Charlie might come from money, but he wasn't in the slightest bit spoiled. He seemed like a really good guy. Vince was a frowning statue, and it annoyed Liz.

Why couldn't he make normal conversation and act like a civil person?

Liz's mother always told her she was too smart and mouthy for her own good. Too much like her father. She said what she thought too often, and it sometimes got her in trouble.

She'd learned to restrain her tongue when she had to, but she felt no obligation to restrain herself at the moment. Vince Darcy was acting like an arrogant jerk when everyone had been nothing but friendly to him.

He deserved to be punished a little.

She leaned forward and gave him a wide smile he couldn't ignore. "Are you happy to be moving back to Abingdon, Vince?"

He blinked at her, clearly surprised by her abrupt question. Charlie and Jane were talking about teaching on the other side of the room, and he'd been vaguely listening to the conversation.

When he didn't reply immediately, she waited, a smile pasted on her face. She wasn't going to let him get away with not responding.

He cleared his throat. "Uh, I guess it will be all right."

"That doesn't sound very positive. Don't you like Abingdon?"

"It's okay."

She wanted to roll her eyes, but she managed to refrain from the impulse. "You were in Blacksburg before? Is that right?"

"Yes." Vince looked like he wanted to be anywhere but here.

She was momentarily struck by the possibility that Emma had suggested—that he was shy. Maybe that was why he looked like he wanted to escape.

That idea cast a much more sympathetic glow on his reluctance to speak, so her expression softened as she said, "I've been to Blacksburg a couple of times. It's a nice town. Did you like it?"

"I did."

"It's too bad you had to give up your job there."

"Yes."

"But it's nice you were able to come back and help your mom with the store."

"Yes."

Okay. This couldn't just be shyness. Most shy people she knew—including her own sister—appreciated people who took the time to talk to them and draw them out.

Liz had been right from the beginning. This man was just rude.

He didn't want to be here. He didn't want to be talking to them. His friend had dragged him over, but he wasn't going to be friendly.

She normally would have given up on a conversation that was going so badly, but Vince didn't deserve to be let off the hook and allowed to sit in silence.

So she pressed on. "So how do you like working at the store?"

His gray eyes were focused on her face, and they were quite unnerving. Deep. Observant. Intelligent. Completely unsmiling. "It's fine."

"I guess you were already in college when your parents moved to Abingdon."

"Yes."

Liz gave him a bright smile as she tried to hide her exasperation. "So what's your favorite thing about working at the store so far?"

Vince was saved from answering the question when Anne stood up. "I'm sorry to break up the party," she said, "but I've got an early start, so I better be getting home."

Anne lived with her sister and brother-in-law in a unit on the ground floor, and she traveled a lot for her work.

Vince practically jumped to his feet as well. "We better be going too."

Charlie stood up much more reluctantly. He'd seemed to be really enjoying Jane's company. "I guess we have to go. It was great to meet you all." To his credit, his smile made the circuit around the room, including all of them, although his gaze lingered longest on Jane.

They all assured him it had been great to meet him too, and it wasn't long before the two men and Anne had left through the front door.

"Well, that's settled," Em announced. "Jane and Charlie."

Liz glanced at her older sister and saw that she was blushing. "Yep. Jane and Charlie. That's a done deal."

"Don't be silly," Jane said.

Em replied, "We're not being silly. We all saw what was going on between you two. He might need some time to get over his breakup, but it will happen as soon as he's ready. And his family is loaded, so just think about how much that will help. Maybe if you marry him, you won't always be talking about selling this place."

One of the first things Liz had suggested when she found out the reality of her family's financial situation was that they sell off this condo in Pemberley House. The mortgage payments were very high, and they certainly didn't need this condo. It had been one of their mother's extravagant, impractical purchases. But their mother wouldn't hear of selling. It was a point of pride to her that they owned one of the condos in Pemberley House. But Liz still kept the possibility in the back of her mind and mentioned it occasionally when she was particularly worried about money.

She loved this place. She wouldn't want to live anywhere else. But if it was a choice between her family business and the Pemberley House condo, the condo would have to be sacrificed.

"I'm not going to marry anyone for money!" Jane's lovely face was outraged.

"I didn't say you should marry him for money," Em replied blithely. "Just that if you happened to fall in love with a rich man, that wouldn't necessarily be a bad thing. So that leaves Vince for Liz. His mother is convinced he needs a wife, and he clearly needs one with a lot of backbone. No one has more backbone than Liz."

"You can forget about that right now." Liz was pleased that her voice was cool and reflected none of the flustered exhilaration she was feeling. "I don't want the stuck-up asshole."

"I saw you torturing the poor guy," Jane said with a reproachful smile.

"I wasn't torturing him, and he isn't a poor guy. I was trying to have a normal conversation with him, and he simply refused. I'm surprised he didn't just yawn in my face and get it over with."

"Give him a chance. If Charlie is his friend, he can't be that bad."

"Charlie is obviously like you and sees the best in everyone, but I'm not like that. I gave Vince Darcy a chance, and he blew it. I don't like him."

"He is good-looking," Em said.

Liz rolled her eyes. "His hotness isn't enough to make up for his personality."

"So you *did* think he was hot." There was a lilt to Em's voice that Liz knew very well. "I knew there was something there. I'm never wrong about pairing people up."

"You were wrong! There's nothing there. Don't even start thinking like that."

Despite the vehemence of her voice, Liz knew that her cheeks were visibly flushing, and she knew her friend was going to notice.

But there was nothing she could do about that.

Meeting Vince still felt like finding that Chippendale, and her body didn't seem to care that he was a jerk.

~

Vince was displeased with the world.

He knew he had nothing to genuinely complain about. Compared to most people, his life was blessed. His family had a lot of money from two successful businesses. He was healthy and physically capable of doing anything he wanted to do. He had good friends and a family who loved him—even if his mother's love was often channeled into fussing over him. He had a great place to live now with a college friend who only rarely got on his nerves.

But he was feeling grumbly anyway, and he'd just made an unpleasant discovery that made his mood even worse. Evidently his mother had been throwing out hints that he needed a wife to anyone of the female persuasion who happened to be around.

It was embarrassing.

He'd been perfectly happy in Blacksburg. Life had been easy, and nothing had troubled him much.

Then his father died—which was more painful than he could have imagined—and he'd had to move to a town where he didn't know anyone but his mother and Charlie.

It felt strange. Uncomfortable. He'd been shy and withdrawn growing up, so he'd never had a lot of friends. He'd thought he'd gotten over that time in his life, but Abingdon was making him feel that way again.

Even sitting in Liz and Jane's living room, he'd felt like an awkward outsider.

So he was in a bad mood when he woke up the next morning at just after seven o'clock, and an early call from his mother had only made it worse. Charlie's family's condo in Pemberley House was incredibly nice, but it had been sitting empty for years. There was quite a bit of work that needed doing to make it comfortably habitable. Plus he needed to unpack all his stuff.

None of that sounded appealing to him as he made himself a cup of coffee and opened the french doors that led out onto the terrace to let in some fresh air.

He stared outside at the wide lawns and flower beds and walking trails of the estate. Despite how large it was, it wasn't that far from Abingdon's downtown area, so it was only a short drive to the store.

He could hear birds singing from the trees outside. The sun glinted around the edges of a big white cloud to the east.

This was a beautiful place.

He was an ungrateful ass to whine about it.

This realization didn't make him feel any better.

"Hey," a voice came from behind him. It was Charlie, walking on the hardwood floors in bare feet. Like Vince, he hadn't yet dressed for the day and was still wearing what he'd slept in.

"Hi."

"Still in a bad mood?" Charlie made a beeline for the pot of coffee Vince had made.

"Eh."

"It won't be as bad as you think."

"What won't?"

"Moving here. Getting to know people."

Vince didn't like people to know that he used to be shy, but Charlie was an exception. "I know. It's fine."

Charlie came over with his cup of coffee to look out through the open doors the way Vince was. "Our neighbors seem pretty nice."

"Uh-huh." Vince's voice was dry, partly to disguise the surge of interest he experienced at the thought of a pair of laughing green eyes and a very female body.

Charlie was a nice guy, but he wasn't much for picking up on subtleties. He didn't see what Vince's sardonic response was hiding. "I thought they were great."

"Kind of silly with their pink champagne and pink walls and all that giggling."

"I didn't notice them giggling."

"You wouldn't since you immediately claimed the pretty one for yourself."

"They were all pretty."

"You know who I'm talking about."

Charlie gave a sheepish smile. Sometimes Vince wondered how it would feel to be as unguarded as his friend. "I don't think I'm ready to dive into a relationship yet, but she is gorgeous, isn't she?"

"Yes. She is. And she seems mostly sensible, which isn't true of all of them."

"Don't be that way. There's got to be one of the other three that you could like."

"Why does there have to be one I could like? You've already claimed the pretty one, so that leaves me with Robert's old girlfriend, the bossy one, or the annoying one."

"The annoying one?" Charlie was frowning now, obviously trying to sort through the women with Vince's descriptions of them to figure out who was who.

41

Vince had found Liz annoying—both yesterday morning and in the evening—but mostly because she hadn't let him think about anything else since he'd first laid eyes on her. He could still vividly picture the smile twitching at the corners of her lush mouth, like she was secretly laughing at him. He could see the graceful arch of her neck and the way her top had shifted occasionally to give him varying glimpses of the curve of her breasts.

He wasn't sure why the picture of her in his mind had his blood rushing this way. He'd been attracted to women before. Many times. The attraction had never left him feeling like this.

Strangely helpless.

And annoyed because of it.

He'd known exactly what she was thinking last night as she kept asking him irritating questions. She was trying to goad him, make him talk. She was having fun with him.

Vince wasn't good around people he didn't know, but he was usually better than he'd been yesterday evening.

From the first time he'd seen her approaching at the estate sale with her confident stride and her direct stare, he'd been fascinated with her. Then seeing her again with all the flowers, as he was stepping off the elevator, had been like a shot of adrenaline, waking up everything sleeping inside him.

Annoying.

It was the only word for it.

"You don't mean Jane's sister, do you? Is she the Annoying One?" Charlie was still trying to work it out.

"Yes. Liz."

"I didn't think she was annoying."

"You didn't talk to her."

"I didn't need to. She seemed nice and smart and friendly. Man, you really are in a bad mood, aren't you?"

Vince took a deep breath, feeling even more like an ass than ever. What the hell was wrong with him? He wasn't nearly as nice as Charlie was, but he was usually nicer than this. "Yeah. Sorry. I'll get over it soon."

He went back to drinking his coffee and staring outside while Charlie sat down and putzed on his phone for a few minutes.

A noise from outside interrupted his reverie. It sounded like humming, so he turned his head toward the sound.

Liz. Walking out onto her terrace. She was obviously dressed for work in a pair of snug capri pants, high-heeled sandals, and a top that emphasized the roundness of her breasts. Her brown hair was thick and wavy, hanging down around her shoulders. She had a watering can in her hand, and she was humming as she watered the flowers in pots on her terrace.

Vince was hit with another wave of attraction, so strong it took his breath.

Then he was hit almost immediately following with a realization of how easily sound traveled from her terrace to his.

Surely she couldn't have heard what he and Charlie had just been saying. She hadn't been outside at that point. Even if her french doors had been open like his, she wouldn't have been able to...

"Who is that?" Charlie asked, jumping to his feet and coming over to the door.

Vince knew he was hoping to see Jane, but Charlie's smile was genuine as he stepped out onto the terrace and said, "Good morning."

Liz turned to look at them with a bright smile. It was the same kind of smile she'd been giving Vince yesterday evening. Intentional rather than truly genuine. "Good morning," she said brightly. "How's the move going?"

"Slowly. All our stuff is still in boxes."

Needless to say, Charlie was the one to answer. Vince was still standing like an idiot, staring at Liz and trying to judge how far a normal speaking voice would travel.

He'd heard her soft humming very clearly from inside.

"What's that you were humming?" Charlie asked.

Liz laughed. "'Pink Sunglasses.' I didn't realize you could hear me." She shifted her eyes suddenly so her gaze met Vince's without wavering. "I hope I wasn't *annoying* you."

With another blithe smile, she waved and walked back into her condo.

Charlie turned with an intake of breath to look at Vince.

Charlie might not be the quickest mind in the world, but he was nobody's fool. And he knew the truth as well as Vince did.

Vince's voice had traveled when he'd been talking to Charlie earlier about Liz and her friends.

He felt a heavy twisting of his gut and a warming of his cheeks as he processed what it meant.

Liz had heard.

She'd *heard*.

THREE

"Are you sure you heard him right?" Jane asked, her pretty face and dark eyes concerned as she met Liz's eyes in the mirror above the bathroom vanity.

Liz raised her eyebrows as she combed out her hair. It was too thick and wavy to do much with. She pulled it back into a low ponytail for work and just left it hanging loose otherwise. It had a tendency to frizz, so it usually looked messy, no matter how many expensive hair products she experimented with.

Jane and Riot's hair was straight and silky. She'd always wished hers was so easy to manage.

Jane was working on her mascara, but she saw and understood her sister's expression. "Don't give me that look. I'm not being naïve. Maybe you didn't hear the whole conversation and misunderstood something."

"I heard the whole conversation, from the moment Charlie got up and said good morning. I didn't misunderstand anything."

Ever since she'd overheard Vince's conversation yesterday, Liz had tried not to stew about it. She didn't like Vince. She didn't care what he thought about her. It shouldn't matter in any way that he'd spoken of her so disparagingly.

That he'd called her the Annoying One.

But she couldn't seem to let it go. It twisted in her gut, even when she wasn't consciously thinking about it. She hated that it bothered her so much, but she couldn't forget it.

She'd told Jane but nobody else. She didn't want her friends constantly dissecting it, as she knew they would.

"But why would he think you were annoying? He'd only met you for a few minutes and you were perfectly friendly."

"He's clearly one of those guys who's too full of himself to appreciate normal friendliness. And remember we met at the estate sale Thursday morning, and I got one of the Brandt paintings he was after. He's probably used to girls swooning all over him, and I didn't. He was snooty about all of us—as if there's anything wrong with pink champagne. Our paint isn't even pink! It's a very sophisticated dusty rose."

"I don't think that's really the point."

"I know. The point is he doesn't matter. I'm totally fine with being the Annoying One if the judgment is coming from that arrogant jerk." She gave Jane a casual smile. "I'm not going to let him spoil the party for me."

Em had decided on the spur of the moment to throw a party tonight—partly to welcome Vince and Charlie into the building and partly because she loved throwing parties. She'd invited the other residents and a few of her other friends from town, so there would be no more than thirty people there and it wasn't likely to get too wild or unruly.

Liz would have been looking forward to it had it not been for the fact that Vince would be there.

She hadn't seen him since their eyes had met across the terraces yesterday morning. He'd been wearing a pair of dark sleep pants and no shirt, and he'd looked obnoxiously sexy. But he'd also looked stricken, so she had no doubts that he realized that she'd overheard him.

Good.

She hoped he was embarrassed. She hoped he felt bad.

She hoped he didn't think it bothered her a lot.

It *didn't* bother her.

She didn't care about his opinion of her.

At all.

"What are you going to wear?" Jane asked. She had her own bathroom attached to her bedroom, but she'd come to Liz's bathroom so they could get ready for the party together.

"I'm not sure. Probably my black capris. I don't want to look like I'm trying too hard."

"Wear the green top with them. It matches your eyes and makes your boobs look fantastic."

The green top was a little too sexy for Liz's mood at the moment, but she nodded anyway. It wouldn't hurt to look sexy even if she wasn't feeling it right now.

"I'm going to wear my blue dress."

"That's perfect. Charlie will be blown away."

Jane blushed slightly.

"Make sure you flirt with him," Liz added after a moment.

"What do you mean?"

"You know what I mean. Try to flirt. Make an effort. Make sure he knows you're into him. Guys are usually wusses at heart, and they need some encouragement—even ones as smitten as Charlie obviously is."

Jane frowned. "He's just coming off a bad breakup, so I don't think he's looking to be serious yet. Anyway, I'm not any good at flirting. I feel like an idiot when I try."

"I know. Me too. But do your best. He might not be ready to be serious, but he's definitely interested in you. You don't have to do anything embarrassing. Just make sure he knows you like him too."

"I'll try."

That was as much as Liz could hope for, so she didn't pursue the topic.

The truth was, she wasn't any better than Jane at flirting. She saw a lot, and she instinctively understood the interactions she observed among other people. But when it came to her own relationships, she wasn't particularly adept at winning men's hearts. She dated fairly regularly, but she hadn't had a serious boyfriend since college. It always felt like she was playing a role when she went out on dates—like she was trying to be someone she wasn't. Someone who laughed at men's jokes and asked wide-eyed questions and secretly wished she was back home in her pajamas watching Netflix.

Sometimes she wondered if she'd always be that way, if she was like Em and would be happier alone.

It was possible.

A lot of guys didn't want a smart woman with a lot of backbone.

Liz was fine with that. She didn't want a guy who didn't want to make an effort.

It would be nice to have sex occasionally, but she could do without if she had to.

A sudden visual of herself in bed with Vince hit her hard and unexpectedly, leaving her flushed and breathless.

She shook the thought away and checked herself out in the mirror. Her hair looked tousled, but it never looked anything else. Her makeup was discreet, and her face looked pretty and natural.

She looked as good as she was likely to look.

"Wear the green top. I bet Vince will start calling you the Sexy One."

Liz rolled her eyes. "Don't be ridiculous."

She was going to wear the green top, however.

~

An hour later, she was dressed in heels, her green, low-cut wrap top, and her favorite black capris that made her butt look good. She was lighting candles in the glass-and-iron hurricanes on Em's terrace.

Em had been a surprise child for her middle-aged parents, and her mother had evidently not wanted the change in lifestyle a child had brought. She'd walked out on the family when Em was three, and it had been Em and her father ever since. He'd had a lucrative legal practice, and he'd inherited money from his own parents, so he and Em were very well off. He'd bought the best unit in Pemberley House the day it went on the market. The southwest unit on the upper floor—four bedrooms, five bathrooms, and a two-story library in the tower on the corner of the mansion.

Liz loved the unit, and she loved Em's sweet but needy father. He was already upstairs in bed with his soundproof headphones so the party wouldn't bother him.

She normally would have been excited about hanging out this evening, but the thought of seeing Vince was making her antsy.

She'd lit the last candle and was staring out at the sun setting over the wide expanse of manicured lawn and blooming gardens when a voice from behind her surprised her so much she jumped.

"Liz."

She whirled around, although she knew who it was even before she saw Vince standing on the terrace a few feet away from her.

He wore a black Oxford and a pair of well-tailored gray trousers. He looked like he'd stepped off the pages of a catalog, and his face was sober as he looked at her.

She forced her nerves into submission so she could give him a blithe smile. "So you *do* know my name." She made sure her tone was light and teasing.

He wasn't going to know that he'd upset her the way he had.

He gazed at her for a long moment without speaking or smiling. "I'm sorry." His eyes dropped on the words.

"For what?"

"You know."

She bit her bottom lip, caught off guard and at a loss for words. She certainly hadn't expected him to confront the issue directly. She never would have imagined he'd apologize.

She had no idea how to respond.

He was waiting for an answer, so she finally found something to say. "You didn't know I could hear."

"No. But I shouldn't have said it anyway. It was…"

She leaned forward unconsciously as he trailed off, trying to follow the words he wasn't saying. "It was what?"

"An asshole thing to say."

She couldn't have said it better herself. Her mind buzzed and her heart pounded and her stomach just wouldn't sit still. "Oh."

"So I'm sorry."

"Oh."

She needed to say something else. Anything else. She needed to not stand here like a stunned statue. He was going to think the whole thing meant more to her than it should. "It's not a big deal. I did get the one Brandt painting, and I just figured you weren't a morning person." She was pleased that her voice sounded light and unconcerned. "Some people are grumpy before they've had their coffee."

His eyes lifted, and his brows drew together like he was trying to see something in her expression.

She didn't want him to see.

She couldn't let him see that this felt serious to her.

She gave a little laugh. "It's really fine. Don't worry about it. I wasn't supposed to hear what you guys were saying, so I'll pretend I never did."

He didn't answer. She wasn't sure why she was surprised. If he didn't have to talk, he didn't. She had no idea what he was thinking.

"Excuse me," she said at last. "I better see if Em needs any more help."

She moved past him quickly and escaped back inside, leaving Vince standing by himself on the terrace.

～

Vince had felt sick to his stomach since yesterday morning. He'd thought he'd feel better after he apologized, but he didn't really.

51

It didn't feel like it had made anything better, and it bothered him more than it should.

He'd been weird and awkward growing up—never knowing what to say to people and usually saying the wrong thing when he tried. He'd only had a few friends, and those were mostly kids he'd grown up with, who were used to the way he was. He'd gone to UVA for college, resolving to be different. He'd pretended to be a different person there. Someone cool and confident and detached. He'd been convincing enough to make friends and to start dating. He'd kept up the act when he moved to Blacksburg and started working, so he'd had a decent social life there too.

But there was something about moving to a new place, one where his mother lived. It turned him into that weird, awkward boy again.

He wasn't comfortable here, and he reverted back into his worst habits—including completely putting his foot in his mouth around women he was attracted to.

Part of him wanted to simply ignore Liz—pretend that nothing had happened and not have to humiliate himself any further by apologizing. But he felt so guilty he knew he couldn't just let it go. Not if he was ever going to get rid of this sick feeling in his gut.

He'd feel better if he believed that Liz had forgiven him, but he was pretty sure she hadn't. She'd smiled and pretended it didn't matter to her, but he wasn't convinced her smile was genuine.

And he had no idea what to do to fix it.

So he felt as stiff and awkward as a boy as he stood against the wall in the huge room while everyone else laughed and chatted around him.

He wished he were anywhere else, even if he couldn't tear his eyes away from Liz's lovely, smiling face.

This unit was incredible. Fourteen-foot ceilings, elaborate plaster work, a breathtaking chandelier, and elegant antique furnishings. It didn't feel like the kind of place where a normal person lived, but it was clear that Em Woodson was indulged by a rich father. She was obviously used to getting her way and supervising other people. Even with the generously hosted party, she was always giving directions about where everyone should go, whom they should be talking to, and what they should be eating and drinking.

He'd called Em the Bossy One, and it was clearer than ever that the appellation was appropriate. She'd walked over to Liz and Anne and was saying something he couldn't hear. But the gesture in his direction was as loud as words.

She was telling them to go over and talk to him since he was standing by himself.

Liz glanced over to him, and their eyes met across the room. She looked away quickly, but not before Vince felt a rush of exhilaration that was becoming far too familiar to him.

Neither Liz nor Anne appeared enthusiastic about talking to him. He wasn't surprised that Anne was reluctant. She'd dated his brother all through college and then dumped him unceremoniously right before Robert was getting ready to propose to her. Vince wasn't sure Robert had ever gotten over the heartache. Naturally, Anne wouldn't be eager to get chummy with Robert's brother.

And Vince obviously knew why Liz didn't want to come chat with him. He was surprised when he saw that Liz allowed Em to drag her over to where he was standing.

"What are you drinking, Vince?" Em asked him with a smile. She was very pretty in a fair, elegant way with a long neck and a graceful posture. Despite her bossiness, her smile was genuine, and she seemed to sincerely care about people. Vince surprised himself by liking her.

"I had the cab. It was excellent."

"I'll get you some more." With a slanting smile for Liz, Em grabbed his glass and walked over to the table set up as a bar.

Liz smothered an annoyed expression and gave him a rueful smile.

"You don't have to talk to me if you don't want," Vince said.

"Of course I do. Em dragged me over here for exactly that purpose."

"Ah. Then you can say something about the weather."

Liz's green eyes glinted briefly. "It was a beautiful day today, wasn't it?"

"Yes, indeed. Very warm."

"And not too humid."

"And the breeze was very pleasant."

"They're saying it might rain tomorrow."

"That's too bad." Despite the rush of blood in his veins, Vince's humor was tickled by the wryness of Liz's tone and expression. "But I suppose we could use the precipitation."

Liz made a sound in her throat that might have been a suppressed laugh. It gave Vince a thrill of victory.

Before he could think of some way to follow up on this success, Em returned with a full glass of wine for him. "What are you all talking about?" she asked with a mischievous expression.

"The weather," Liz said.

"The weather," Vince said at exactly the same time.

Em chuckled. "Sounds stimulating."

She was starting to say something else when Liz elbowed her. "Look who showed up."

Vince turned in the direction Liz nodded to see a man standing in the entryway by himself, dressed in jeans and a camp shirt. He looked to be in his mid- to late thirties, and he was giving the room a leisurely once-over.

Em visibly perked up. "I can't believe he came! I better go grab him before he changes his mind and leaves." She hurried across the room toward the man.

Vince gave Liz a questioning look.

"That's Ward Knightley. His family used to own this house and estate."

"Oh. Yeah. He's the one who still manages the property?"

"Yep. He lives in one of the cottages. He's a really nice guy, but this isn't exactly his crowd, so Em wasn't expecting him to come."

"She's into him?"

Liz shook her head. "No. Nothing like that. She's known him since she was a little girl. He's like family to her, I think. She treats him like an older brother."

Vince glanced over to Em's face as she greeted the man, and he wondered if that assessment was entirely accurate. But it wasn't his business, and he could be wrong.

It didn't matter anyway—not when Liz was looking at him with something other than veiled contempt.

"Are you interested?" Liz asked.

He blinked. "In what?"

She nodded over toward Em and Ward Knightley.

His eyes widened. "In Em, you mean?"

"Yes. You were asking a lot of questions, and you haven't seemed to be interested in anything else since you've gotten here. So I was wondering." Her eyes met his in what was almost a challenge, as if she were daring him to reply honestly.

"Are you always this direct?"

"Yes. Why shouldn't I be? Are you embarrassed about who you're interested in?"

"I'm not interested in her." He was thrown completely off-balance by this conversation, so he couldn't think of anything to say but the truth.

"Really?"

"Yes, really. I just asked a couple of questions. She's not my type."

"Then what's your type?"

Vince opened his mouth to reply but then closed it again because the truth was he didn't know the answer to her question.

He'd dated all kinds of women in the past. He'd liked women of all varieties. He hadn't liked any of them enough to get serious, but he genuinely didn't know what type of woman he liked the best.

"You aren't going to answer?" she asked, her expression both playful and confrontational in a mingling that was absolutely enchanting.

He couldn't tell her he didn't know what his type was, so he settled for something else. "No. I'm not going to answer. Hasn't anyone ever told you it's not polite to go around demanding what a man's type is?"

"I didn't think you cared about politeness."

"Why do you say that?"

"Because you've been rude every single time I've met you."

"I have?" He knew he'd been unforgivable in what he'd said about her, but he wasn't sure what else he'd done that would have been rude.

Her eyes widened into saucers. "Yes, of course you have! Do you really not know?"

"No," he admitted, unable to look away. "I don't know."

Her eyes were holding his gaze too, and her cheeks flushed slightly. "Well, you have."

"I have?"

"Yes." Her voice was slightly breathless. "You have."

He'd lost track of the conversation as he was washed with a flood of attraction and desire. Her full lips were gracefully curved and expressively agile. He wanted to feel them against his mouth, his skin, his body. Her eyes were both laughing and intelligent and full of such depth that he felt like he could drown in the substance of her personhood.

It was the oddest feeling. To be as drawn to a woman's spirit as he was to her body.

He tilted his head down toward hers. "I'm not sure what I can do about that," he murmured, startled when his voice was huskier than it should have been.

"You can..." She swallowed and licked her lips. "You can... not be rude."

"I'll try not to be." He wasn't going to be able to hold back anymore. He was going to kiss her right now, right here, right in front of the crowded room.

"Lizzie! Lizzie!" The voice came from a far corner but sounded like it was approaching them.

It broke them both out of the moment. Liz turned to look, and her face changed when she saw her younger sister.

Riot.

He'd never really liked Riot, and he definitely didn't appreciate seeing her now.

He'd been so close to kissing Liz, and he knew it would have been good.

But it wouldn't have been smart.

Liz didn't even really like him, so there was no point in liking her too much.

~

Liz woke up every morning for the next week thinking about Vince.

It was more than a little annoying.

Things should feel settled with him now. He'd apologized, and they'd had a mostly civil conversation at the party on Saturday night. She should be able to put him out of her mind, assured that he wasn't going to trouble her again.

It didn't exactly work that way, however.

She had a habit of sitting on her terrace in the mornings, drinking coffee and preparing herself mentally for the day. And every morning she would see him leave for work, striding determinedly from the building to his car, wearing expensive, professional clothes and carrying a travel mug. So then she'd end up thinking about him, wondering what kind of mood he was in and how he was adjusting to working in the store with his mother.

He left for work at about seven every morning, and he came back around six. She knew because three times that week she'd been hanging out with Jane or Em on her terrace at exactly the time he was coming back home.

He would give them a brief wave when he saw them, but he never lingered. He certainly never came over to hang out with them.

Which was fine. It was perfectly normal. After all, people weren't usually best friends with their neighbors. But Charlie found reason to drop by three times during the week—once right at dinnertime so he'd been invited to join them—and Vince never did.

Just more proof that Liz should put him out of her mind for good.

If he'd had any interest in getting to know them (*her*), he would have made more of an effort.

Her mind wouldn't cooperate. When she was lying in bed at night, she'd be hit with visions of his sober gaze, his fine shoulders, the fire that had smoldered in his eyes as he'd leaned closer to her on Saturday at the party, as if he was about to kiss her hard.

She'd play movies in her imagination of how things might have gone had Riot not called out for her just then. Then she'd make up stories about how they might run into each other again. What he would say. What she would say.

How he would kiss her for real.

It was all highly disturbing, and Liz wished she was more in control of herself. She wasn't usually like this, and she didn't like it.

So at eight thirty on Saturday morning, a week after the party, she was sitting on her terrace, drinking coffee and playing on her phone and trying not to wonder how late Vince slept in on Saturdays.

She was almost relieved when the doors opened behind her and Riot came out to flop down in the chair beside her, wearing her purple fleece pajamas and a grumpy expression. She'd spent the night with Liz and Jane last night, as she occasionally did when she wanted to get away from their parents.

Riot's real name was Harriet, but she'd always hated it, so she'd renamed herself Riot in middle school and the name had stuck.

"It's kind of early for you to be up, isn't it?" Liz asked.

"Jane woke me up banging around in her room."

This was obviously the source of the bad mood. Liz shook her head. "She's moving the furniture around in her room."

"By herself?"

"I helped her with the bed and dresser."

"And y'all couldn't wait until noon or some other reasonable time of the day?"

"Jane has to cover the shop today starting at ten. And, if I recall, you have to go into Darcy's by ten today too."

"I know. I hate working Saturdays. I hate sitting around watching stupid people eyeball every item in the store and then finally decide to buy nothing but a fifty-cent spoon."

Liz gave a huff of amusement since she'd felt the same impatience herself many times. "I know. But you can quit any time you want and find a different sort of job. You just took the job at Darcy's to spite Mom and Dad anyway."

"They told me I had to get a job if I wanted to keep living with them, so I got one."

Riot was still in college and still living with their parents. She'd failed out of UVA her sophomore year, so her parents had brought her back home, insisting that if she was going to live off them, she had to take classes toward a degree at a local college and get some sort of job.

So Riot had taken the job at Darcy's just to piss everyone off. She was twenty-two now and still doing it.

"You could always work for Mom and Dad like me and Jane," Liz added.

"I would, but you get all the good stuff to do. Why can't I help with the buying?"

"If you'd taken the time to get educated on art and antiques like I have so you could recognize what's valuable and what's not, then you could have helped with the buying. But you never learned, so you'd come back with a bunch of worthless junk."

"I would not."

"You would too." Liz never coddled her younger sister the way the rest of her family did. Doing so just made Riot act more like a baby, and she already acted more like a fourteen-year-old than a twenty-two-year-old. "You don't know anything about antiques. You could never acquire good inventory, and you can't do the accounting or administration like Jane. So if you want to help with the store, you'll have to work the shop. Your other choice is to find a different job doing anything you like and support yourself."

Riot grumbled under her breath, an obvious sign of exactly what she thought of that idea.

She wasn't actually much of an arguer, and long experience had taught them both that Liz would win any argument between them based on reason and evidence. Riot's strategy was to whine ceaselessly until people gave up and gave her what she wanted.

Liz hated that her sister was so immature, and part of her wished her parents would finally put their foot down with her and kick her out of the house so she would have no choice but to grow up. But they hadn't yet, and Riot showed no signs of maturing anytime soon.

"Maybe you can take me with you sometime when you're buying," Riot said after a minute. "You could teach me."

Liz's first instinct was to give that suggestion a decided no, but she bit back the word. Riot had been spoiled, and she would never learn to be a functioning part of the family business until they gave her the opportunity. "I can take you sometime, but we'd have to start with the flea markets and estate sales."

"But I wanted to—"

"I can't take you with me to an auction because the pace is too fast. You'd distract me and slow me down, and then we'd miss out on the best pieces. I'm hitting a couple of flea markets first thing tomorrow morning. You can come with me if you want."

"Okay." Riot looked almost excited.

"We have to get there early to get the good stuff. I'll be leaving at six thirty tomorrow morning."

"Six thirty!"

"You said you wanted to learn buying."

Riot mumbled something. Liz figured there was no more than a fifty percent chance of Riot actually waking up in time to go with her tomorrow.

Before either of them could say anything else, Jane came out onto the terrace with a bottle of water. She wore skinny jeans and a tank top that made her look as slim and graceful as a model. Her face was flushed, and her hair was pulled up into a messy ponytail.

"Did you get it done?"

"Yes. I think so. I like it better this way. I can see the view outside from the bed."

"Are you thinking someone else is going to be seeing the view from your bed soon?" Riot asked.

Liz rolled her eyes, and Jane shook her head.

"Well? You like him, don't you?"

"Hush," Jane whispered, looking back at the terrace for Vince and Charlie's unit. The french doors were closed, but still.

Liz had good reason to know that voices carried.

Jane met her eyes. "I'm going to get that floor lamp out of storage. You know that one with the stained-glass globe?"

"Oh yeah. That would look great in your room."

"Do you know where it is in the storeroom? That place is chaos."

"Yeah. It's kind of in the middle. It's got a bunch of boxes around it, so you'll need to—" Liz stood up. "You know what? I better come with you. Let me throw on some clothes."

"You don't have to—"

"It's going to be hard for you to move all the stuff out of the way on your own. I don't mind. I'm just sitting here doing nothing anyway. Just give me a minute to put something on, and I'll be ready."

FOUR

Vince dumped his remaining coffee in the sink and put his mug into the dishwasher before turning back to face Charlie, who was wrapping thick brown paper around the large terrarium he'd spent the past week making.

"Why did you have to make it so big?" Vince asked, taking in the large form and trying to imagine the pain it was going to be to carry it down to the car, drive it over to the school, and install it into Charlie's third-grade classroom.

The collection of plants in Charlie's class was getting a very fancy new home.

"Well, I didn't mean to, but I kept thinking of new plants to add, so it got bigger and bigger." Charlie's face was rueful but also pleased. He looked like a kid with a new toy. "The kids are going to love it."

"Not just the kids," Vince said dryly. "The only ones who are going to remain unimpressed are the plants themselves."

Charlie laughed as he taped up the protective paper with an abundance that wasn't entirely necessary. "The plants will love it too."

"Well, hurry up and finish with the tape so we can haul the thing to the school."

"I'm all done."

The two men stared at the covered terrarium for a few seconds, and Vince silently prayed that they'd be able to get the monstrosity across town and into place without a calamity.

Charlie and his students would be very upset if it were to fall and bust apart.

After plotting out a course of action, the two of them carried the terrarium to the elevator and then out of the building without incident. It was heavy, but the main obstacle was its awkward bulk. They were maneuvering it into the back of Vince's SUV, since it wouldn't fit into Charlie's ancient Mustang, when another car pulled into the lot not far from them.

Vince recognized it immediately, and his senses went into high alert.

He'd spent the entire past week—ever since the party—trying to feel normal again, like his regular self.

He was settling in at his mother's store and finding the work interesting and surprisingly satisfying. He was getting along well with Charlie, despite their close quarters and the fact that Vince wasn't really a roommate kind of person. He was enjoying the time with his mother and convinced his presence was helping her through her grief.

Overall, things in his life were evening out, and he should start to feel like himself again.

But he didn't.

And something about Liz was responsible.

He didn't understand it, and he didn't like it, but he couldn't stop thinking about her. He'd on purpose tried to avoid her all week, but he saw her in passing fairly often and every time was like a blast of cold air, waking him up when he hadn't even known he'd been sleepwalking.

It happened again now as he saw her car pulling into one of her unit's assigned parking places.

He was bent over, reaching in to fit the damned terrarium into the back seat, and he wished his position wasn't quite so undignified.

"What is that thing?" Liz called out. She must have gotten out of her car based on the location and clarity of her voice, but Vince's head was still trapped in the back of the car, trying to move the monstrosity into position without ripping his leather upholstery.

"It's a terrarium," Charlie explained, straightening up. It sounded like he was grinning, while Vince was still straining to get the thing to move into place. "For my classroom."

"Oh fun!" That was Liz.

"Nice." Jane had evidently gotten out of the car too since Vince recognized her voice.

"We all must have been hit with the moving bug this morning since Jane and I are doing the same thing. We just got a lamp and an end table out of our storage unit." Liz sounded bright and pleasant, and Vince really wanted to see her face, her expression.

He wanted it so much he didn't let himself straighten up. He hadn't gotten the terrarium secure on the seat yet anyway.

"Oh, if you're moving furniture, hold on a minute, and Vince and I will help," Charlie volunteered.

"Thank you, but we're fine," Jane said in her low, slightly detached voice. "They're not very heavy, and you look busy."

Her response gave Vince a different kind of prickle in his mind. This one worry. Charlie was already totally gone on Jane, and he was afraid Jane didn't feel the same way. She was always very nice, but also distanced, as if she wasn't taking her interaction with Charlie nearly as seriously as he was.

Vince didn't want to see his friend get hurt, and he was increasingly afraid it was going to happen.

"Charlie," he said, his voice more abrupt than he'd intended. "I need some help here, and if my leather gets damaged, you're going to pay for it."

"Oh. Yeah. Sorry." Charlie turned toward his side of the back seat. "Hold on a minute, and we'll help y'all with your stuff."

Vince was pretty sure Liz wasn't going to want to feel like a helpless weakling, so he didn't think she'd be waiting for the men's help.

He was right.

By the time Vince and Charlie had gotten the terrarium in place and closed the doors, Liz was carrying a tall floor lamp with a stained-glass globe, and Jane was carrying a small end table.

Neither piece could be very heavy. Surely they'd be fine getting the furniture into their place on their own.

Vince was flushed and hot and sweating and irritable and worried about Charlie and infuriatingly drawn to Liz's lovely face, her expression reflecting a wry amusement as if she understood exactly how Vince was feeling.

He wasn't used to people reading him so easily.

It rankled at him.

He was about to tell Charlie to get into the car so they could get going when Jane suddenly went down. Since Vince was looking in her direction, he saw it happen.

The sidewalks on the estate were all done with historic pavers, many of them original. They were beautiful but also uneven in places, and Jane's foot landed on a particularly uneven spot.

Her ankle turned, and she fell, the end table landing on top of her already twisted foot.

Jane cried out in obvious pain, and Liz made a startled sound and ran over, putting down the lamp so she could crouch beside her sister. Charlie ran over too, his face distraught with worry.

"Are you all right?" Vince asked, genuinely concerned. The fall had looked painful. That ankle wasn't going to be good.

Jane's face was white, and her skin was wet with perspiration. She tried to speak, but only a whimper came out.

Charlie had taken charge of the end table, and Liz was inspecting her sister's ankle. She moved it gently, and Jane cried out sharply in response.

"It's more than just a twisted ankle," Liz said, sounding as serious as Vince had ever heard her. "I think I better take her to the emergency room to get it x-rayed."

Jane nodded, biting down on her lower lip.

"Vince and I will take you," Charlie said, already starting to help get Jane to her feet.

She couldn't put any weight on the ankle, so Liz and Charlie propped her up between them as they made their way to Liz's small, inexpensive sedan. Vince would have volunteered his vehicle, but there was a gargantuan terrarium in his back seat.

He could see how determined Charlie was to help out Jane, but Vince was worried that they would be more hassle than help.

Liz confirmed this worry because, as soon as they got Jane into the front seat of the car, she turned toward Vince and Charlie. "Y'all really don't have to go with us."

"Of course we do," Charlie insisted. "You'll need help with Jane, and we can keep you company while you wait. It always takes hours in the emergency room."

Vince knew that to be true, but he met Liz's eyes and said softly, "Tell us if you don't want us to tag along."

Liz seemed to understand. Her face relaxed slightly. "I don't mind. Really. I just don't want you to feel obliged. I'm sure it's the last thing you want to do on a Saturday."

"My other choice was hauling that terrarium, so honestly this is better."

Liz's lips turned up slightly in a smile that wasn't bright but still looked sincere.

He couldn't help but respond to it. "We're happy to help with your sister."

His conclusion was obviously irrelevant to Charlie, who was already climbing into the back seat of Liz's car and talking the whole time to Jane.

Liz and Vince walked around to the other side and got in.

Vince wasn't feeling at all like himself. Something was moving inside his chest, his belly. Flapping. Flying.

Fluttering.

He hoped it would go away soon.

~

An hour later, Liz walked out into the waiting room to find that Charlie and Vince were sitting in a far corner, away from everyone else.

The emergency room hadn't been very crowded, but everything at a hospital seemed to take forever. Liz had held Jane's hand as they waited to be called for, and then she'd gone back with her sister as they waited a long time for a doctor to make an appearance.

"How is she?" Charlie asked, jumping out of his seat as she approached.

"She's fine. They gave her something for the pain. The doctor thinks it's just a sprain, but they're taking her to get an X-ray to make sure nothing is broken. Then they'll know if she needs a cast or anything. They kicked me out. They said it might be a couple of hours, so you guys can leave if you want to."

She knew immediately that Charlie wouldn't want to leave, but she was worried about Vince resenting having his whole day wasted like this. She didn't want him to stay if he'd rather be somewhere else.

"Of course we're not going to leave," Charlie said. "We can keep you company."

Liz met Vince's eyes. He'd stood up too at her approach, and his face was sober but not as aloof as she'd seen it before. "It's no problem at all," he said softly.

"Okay. Thanks. Hopefully it won't take forever." She sat down in an empty seat and then realized it was the one right beside Vince.

He sat down too.

He smelled good. Clean and faintly expensive but still natural. Like a real person. She breathed him in without conscious volition.

"Do you need something to drink?" Charlie asked. "Or eat? Maybe Jane will be hungry when she comes out. Do you think I should get something for her?"

He was so obviously worried that Liz's heart went out to him, but she also knew the man was going to drive her crazy if he acted like this for an hour or two as they waited.

So she thought for a minute and then said, "You know, that's not a bad idea. She loves the chicken salad sandwiches from Stella's. Since we have plenty of time, if you don't mind, maybe you could run out and get some. You could take my car."

"That's a great idea. I'll do that. Do you want one too?"

"That would be great. And here, let me give you some money. You can get something for you and Vince too."

"I'm not going to take your money. I'll get stuff for everyone and be back as soon as I can." Charlie took the keys Liz offered him.

"Please don't hurry," Liz told him as he turned to leave the waiting room. "We have plenty of time."

When he'd disappeared through the doors, Vince gave a huff of something that sounded like amusement.

She turned to check his expression.

"That was pretty smart," Vince murmured. "Giving him something to do. Otherwise, he'd keep driving us crazy."

"He's worried," Liz said with a smile she couldn't quite hold back. "He's a really nice guy."

"He is. He's a good friend."

"How long have you known him?"

"Since college. He lived in the room next door to mine. When I decided to move to Abingdon, I remembered he lived here, so I looked him up and discovered he was getting ready to move into Pemberley House, so it worked out for us to share a place."

Liz nodded, wondering what Vince had been like in college, wondering how someone as aloof as Vince had become friends with someone as open and earnest as Charlie.

"So was your sister really feeling better, or did you just say that to relieve Charlie's mind?"

"No, she really did seem a bit better. It must have hurt like hell at first because I've never seen her so pale."

"I saw she was squeezing your hand on the drive over," Vince said. "I'm surprised you were able to drive one-handed."

"Fortunately it was an easy drive. I didn't want to pull my hand away since she seemed to need it." Liz sighed. "Poor Jane."

"She's pretty brave. A lot of people would have been moaning and crying. You should have seen the dramatics the guys on my soccer team would go into when they were injured."

Liz felt strangely validated by Vince's words, even though they were affirming Jane and not her. "She is brave, and she never goes into dramatics. But she was probably more stoic than usual because you and Charlie were there."

"Why should that matter? We wouldn't have cared if she cried."

"Maybe, but people always put on a different face around other people than they do around family." She slanted him a look, relieved when he met her eyes seriously. He appeared to be really listening, thinking about what she said.

"Another face?"

"Yes. You know what I mean, don't you? You've got your real face and then the face you show to the rest of the world. The face you show to the rest of the world is always a little... better than your real face. More pulled together, more smart or funny or nice or in control or whatever it is you want yourself to be. You might want that outward face to be you, but it never quite is."

Vince's expression changed in a way she didn't quite understand. His lips softened. His eyes deepened. "I thought it was just me who did that."

"Of course it's not just you. I think everyone does it. You put on your best face for the world and only show your real one to the people closest to you. Family or whatever."

"Who do you show your real face to?"

She slanted him a quick look, her cheeks warming for no good reason. "My family. Em and Anne. No one else."

"No boyfriends?"

She shook her head, oddly excited by the intimate conversation that had come out of nowhere. "Not right now. But even when I've had boyfriends, I've never shown them my real face." She paused. Hesitated. But she'd always prided herself at speaking her mind, and she wasn't going to stop doing so now. "What about you? Who do you show your real face to?"

Vince didn't answer immediately. He stared at a spot in the air in front of him, his gray eyes blank and his jaw muscles rippling with tension. Finally he said very softly, "I'm not sure I show it to anyone."

"What about your mom?"

"Maybe her."

"Your brother?"

"We used to be close, but I haven't spent much time with him for years. He always lives half a world away."

Liz nodded and didn't know what to say. It was very unusual for her, but it felt like Vince had burdened her with the weight of knowledge she wasn't really ready for.

Like she now knew more about him than she should be allowed.

Finally she asked in a tone that was almost gentle, "What's so wrong with your real face?"

He didn't answer immediately. He didn't meet her eyes. "I... don't know. I don't think anything's wrong with it—except it's not who I want to be. My mom says that I live life on the surface. That I never go deep. Maybe she's right."

There was nothing she could say. Nothing that could match the weight of what he'd just told her.

She wanted to match it, to meet it, to show him that she was taking him seriously. She had to think a long time before she had something to say. "Maybe... maybe your friends and family know your real face anyway. They can see it... see it beneath the other face. People who know us well usually can. It sounds like your mom can anyway."

"Probably."

"And if you don't like something about yourself, you can always try to change."

"Yeah." Vince turned suddenly to meet her eyes with an unexpected quirk of his lips. "How did we land in this particular conversation?"

She laughed, relieved that the intensity of the moment before was over and disappointed at the same time. "I have no idea. Must have been a temporary aberration."

"Must have been." He paused and then asked in a different tone. "Are you going to call your folks about Jane?"

"Yes. I will eventually. But I'd rather she be done with the doctor and back home before I do."

"Why is that?"

"Because if I call now, they'll all come right over here and it will be... a big production."

"What do you mean a production?"

"I mean, my family isn't exactly laid-back, and everything becomes a big deal. My mom would arrive and talk nonstop about how upset she is and how hard it's going to be for Jane to deal with a sprained ankle and how attractive the doctors and nurses are and which one is likely to ask Jane out." Vince chuckled at that, so Liz went on. "And Riot would come too and try to make sure all the attention is on her. She'd end up doing something embarrassing like hitting on a doctor. You know her, right? You know what she's like. And my dad would be making sarcastic comments about everyone and pretending he didn't care about what was going on. It would be a production. Better to wait until everything is settled and we're out of here before I call them."

"So your mom is kind of like Riot?"

"Yes. They're actually a lot the same. Riot is still growing up, but she'll probably be a lot like my mom when she finally does it. I'm kind of like my dad, although I'm more of a go-getter than he is."

"So who is Jane like?"

Liz had to think about that. "I'm not sure. She looks like my mom, but her personality is not like either one of our parents."

"Interesting."

"Are you like your mom or your dad?"

"Much more like my dad." Vince's expression changed, and Liz suddenly remembered that he'd lost his father just a few months ago.

"You miss him?" she asked lightly.

He nodded, staring now at a spot on the floor. "Yeah. A lot more than I thought I would."

"Yeah. I guess it's always like that, isn't it?"

"Yeah."

It felt like they understood each other in a way they hadn't before, and the thrill of it made her blood surge through her veins. When she looked over at him, she saw that he was looking at her.

Their eyes met.

The look deepened.

She felt herself leaning toward him.

It was kind of like last week at the party, when she'd thought for sure he would kiss her. But this was more than that. More than attraction. More than chemistry.

It was an intimacy she'd never dreamed she'd share with Vince. An intimacy she'd never felt before.

Vince's eyes had warmed, and she was sure once again that he would kiss her.

She wanted it so much.

"I'm back!" Charlie. Returning far too soon with the sandwiches.

Everything changed after that. Went back to normal.

It was fine. Better. Definitely safer.

But kind of crushing just the same.

~

Two hours later, Charlie was helping Jane in through the front door of their unit, and Vince and Liz were walking behind them.

"You can just help me to the couch," Jane said, sounding tired and weak but as composed as she always was. "I'm supposed to elevate my ankle."

It was a bad sprain but not a break, which was good news in terms of healing.

Liz was relieved the ordeal was over and hadn't been as bad as it could have been.

Things had been a lot better because Charlie and Vince had come along.

"Do you need anything?" Vince asked softly, his eyes on Charlie as his friend lowered Jane to the couch.

"No. Thanks. We'll be just fine now. I appreciate you both helping out." Without thinking, Liz reached out and put a hand on his forearm.

Vince looked down at her fingers on his skin. His expression was unreadable. "It was no problem. We were happy to help. Just let us know if you need anything."

He seemed kind of stiff now, and she suspected he might have regretted being so open in their conversation earlier.

As he'd admitted to her, he wasn't the kind of person who usually let people in. And she wasn't his friend. Or anything to him.

No wonder he seemed silent and awkward and like he wanted to get out of there.

She wasn't going to hold him back.

Part of her might want a renewal of that intimacy, but if he didn't want it, she wasn't going to push.

It wasn't like she really liked him or anything.

He was just interesting. A strange kind of challenge. And, yes, ridiculously attractive, but that was never the most important thing.

Not to Liz anyway.

"Come on, Charlie," Vince said more forcefully. "We need to get out of their hair now. Give them some peace."

Charlie said a few more things to Jane before he reluctantly walked over to the door. "Call us if she needs anything," he said to Liz.

"I will. And thanks to you both. We really appreciate it." Liz was smiling, but she was feeling weird now too, so she was as relieved as Vince when the men finally disappeared through the door.

"Are you okay?" Jane asked from the couch, when Liz stood and stared at the closed door for too long.

"Yes. I'm fine. Do you need anything?"

"No. Not now." Jane gave her a sharp look. "So you like Vince now, do you?"

Liz stiffened. "Of course not!"

"It kind of looks like you do."

"Well, I don't. Not really. He's not as bad as I originally thought, but I'm still the Annoying One to him, remember? And he's the kind of man who never lets himself get close to people, so a girl would be pretty dumb to fall for him. He might be okay for a hot fling. But he's not boyfriend or husband material."

Jane didn't look convinced, but she also didn't argue, so Liz was able to let the subject drop.

What she'd said was true. Vince had told her straight out that he didn't let people in.

And he obviously wasn't going to change that with her.

Best to just forget about him and move on with her life.

FIVE

A month later, Liz was headed for another estate sale at five thirty in the morning.

She'd left earlier this time just in case Vince was planning to attend too.

She wanted to be first in line.

Out of principle.

This was the first estate sale she'd attended since the one six weeks ago when she'd first met Vince. She'd been to a couple of auctions, including one last weekend where she'd encountered Vince. He'd come over to sit by her, and they'd chatted casually. She'd expected to have to compete for the best pieces—something that made the whole thing more exciting to her—but he'd been fairly laid-back.

She'd finally realized he was mostly just learning how those kinds of auctions worked, getting used to the pace and system so he could operate in them in the future.

It was hard to feel a genuine rivalry in such a situation, so she'd just enjoyed his company instead.

They saw each other fairly often now.

Charlie had devoted himself to helping Jane with her sprained ankle, and he was still taking her anywhere she wanted to go and bringing dinner in a few times a week. That threw Liz and Vince together more often than they would have been otherwise.

She felt like she knew him now. She was used to him. But it wasn't like they were friends.

He still maintained that aloofness he'd had the whole time except for a few minutes in the hospital waiting room. She'd come to the conclusion that he wasn't really as rude as she'd assumed at the beginning but also that he held people at arm's length.

She was just as attracted to him as she'd ever been, but she was trying to talk herself out of that.

She'd done a pretty good job overall.

The only real slipup in the past month was two weeks ago. She'd been reading on a lounge chair in her favorite spot in the gardens when Vince had passed by on his run. He was in really good shape and ran nearly every day. He'd paused, running in place when she'd said hello.

He'd asked what she was reading—a cozy mystery—and then they'd ended up talking about books for almost an hour, right there in the garden.

She hadn't realized he was a reader, but he was, and his reading was much wider than hers—ranging from literary classics to popular "book club" books. His dry commentary on their flaws amused her, even as she teased him about approaching books the same way he did people. He never let himself go all the way in with his emotions.

It had been the best part of her week. That conversation about books with Vince. At the end of it, when they'd gotten to their feet to leave, she'd said, "One day you need to read a book and just let yourself go."

He'd taken a step closer and met her eyes. "How does one let oneself go in a book?"

"You stop separating yourself from the characters and story. You stop analyzing and judging and figuring things out. You just feel what the characters feel. You live with them. Feel with them."

Somehow she'd gotten backed up against a tree, and Vince was leaning into her. She'd been brutally aware of him as a man, as a human being. The heat radiating from him. The smell of his skin. The tension in his muscles. She hadn't been able to look away.

"Feel with them?" he'd murmured, thicker than normal.

"Yes. Feel with them. Just... just..." She'd been breathless and pulsing with excitement and need.

Vince had been so close. She could reach out and touch him. He could lean forward and claim her lips with his.

"Just what?" he'd asked.

"Just let go."

The words sounded almost like a plea. Like she was begging him to kiss her, take her, let go completely with her.

She'd suddenly heard herself and cringed at the sound of them.

Vince had done nothing—nothing—to indicate real interest in her, other than maybe a superficial attraction that matched hers. And she was practically panting over him in an embarrassing way that wasn't at all like her.

So she'd cleared her throat and added, "That's how you let go with books. You should think about it."

Vince had stepped back. His breathing was fast and shallow, although it had been an hour since he'd been running. "Ah. Got it."

And that had been it. The only time she'd slipped up in the past month.

She'd learned her lesson after that since the next time she saw Vince he'd basically ignored her.

She wasn't going to be stupid about him. She was far too smart for that.

But she was still overly excited as she drove the half hour to the estate sale that morning. It was a good sale with a lot of items of potential value, although there wasn't anything in particular that she was dying to get the way she'd been those Brandt paintings.

And there was a good chance Vince would be there.

She was going to beat him this morning.

She took the turn into the driveway and held her breath as she approached the large house. Then she let it out and smiled when she discovered there were no other cars in the parking area or along the driveway.

No fancy dark gray SUV.

She'd gotten here before Vince.

She parked her car, put her keys in her purse, and dug out her pad of sticky notes, getting herself organized. Before she'd done so, she heard a car approaching.

A quick glance beside her proved her immediate fear.

Vince.

He was here already, and she wasn't yet out of her car.

She jumped out as Vince was putting his SUV in park, and their eyes met through his windshield.

She started walking fast, not wanting to run since it might look silly and undignified.

But she was going to be first in line this time.

She was halfway to the door when she became aware that Vince was behind her.

He had to know what she was thinking.

He was doing this on purpose.

He was trying to beat her just to prove that he could.

She ran. Flat out. As fast as she could.

Vince was chuckling as he picked up his pace, but there was no way Liz was going to let him win. She was moving so fast she couldn't slow her momentum enough, so she slammed into the front doorframe with more force than she would have wanted.

But she'd made it first.

She let out a cry of victory, whirling around and raising her arms in triumph.

Vince was out of breath like she was, but he was still laughing, low in his throat, his expression warm and relaxed in a way she'd never seen it before.

His smile was a real one.

He was having a good time.

That fact went right to her head.

"Are you always this competitive?" he asked, accepting his second-place status without grudge.

She had to catch her breath before she responded, and she used the time to write a One on the first sticky note for her and a great big Two on the second one for Vince.

She handed it to him with a grin. "You're the one who started running to try to beat me to the door when I was clearly here first."

"Hey, it's not my fault you were slow." He took his Two and slapped it on his shirt like an ironic badge of honor. "But I was mostly just trying to get you going."

"You did get me going. There was no way I was going to let you win this time."

"Being first in line isn't really winning."

"It's winning at this moment."

He laughed again. "So back to my question. Are you always this competitive, or is it just me who brings it out?"

"Oh, I'm always this way. Ask anyone. My sisters refused to play board games with me as kids because I always took them too seriously."

"I can imagine. Did you burst into tears every time you lost?"

"No! Of course not. I almost never lost, but when I did, I demanded an immediate redo of the game and made sure I won the second time."

Vince was leaning against the other side of the doorframe, giving her a smile that was almost fond. "No wonder they gave up on playing with you. Did you ever play sports?"

"Yeah. I swam on a swim team and played basketball in high school. I was good."

"I bet you were. You didn't play in college?"

"No. I wasn't top tier or anything, and honestly college sports take up too much time. I was already working with my dad in the store when I started college, so I didn't have much time for extracurriculars."

"Was that because you wanted to or because *he* wanted you to?"

"Eh. Both, I guess. My mom has great taste and loves antiques, and she's really good with customers, but she doesn't have a head for business, so my dad was very happy when Jane and I got old enough to help so he didn't have to do it all. But I've loved the store ever since I was tiny. I used to explore for hours, feeling like I was searching for treasure. So it was what I wanted to do too."

"Have you never thought about moving away? Doing something entirely different?"

"I've thought about it. But what I love most are antiques. So if I had to move, I'd try to find a similar sort of job. Why would I do that when I already have the job I love the most."

"And you don't mind working with your family?"

"No. Why would I?"

"I don't know. It just seems like most people want to get away eventually."

She shrugged, wondering if he thought she was childish or unnatural for never trying to get distance from her family. "Maybe. But I have no reason to. It's not like I live in the same house as my parents. We can live in the same town and work together, and I can still have enough distance. I don't need hundreds of miles between us. Besides, they need me. I'm not going to just walk out on them."

Vince didn't say anything, and his expression looked interested but not skeptical, so he must not think she was too strange.

"I guess you never would have moved close to your mom if you hadn't needed to," Liz said.

Vince's mouth twisted slightly. "I wasn't that far away from her to begin with. Blacksburg is less than two hours away."

"I know. I just meant you wouldn't have moved to the same town and started working with her if you'd had a choice."

"I did have a choice. You really think I'm a selfish bastard?"

"No. Sorry. No. I didn't mean it to sound that way. I was just thinking we're different, and that's one of the ways it shows. You came back when you needed to, but I never left."

She wasn't sure why she was even talking about this, and it was making her self-conscious. So she shut up.

Vince was quiet too.

They stood in the silence of the morning for a few minutes, occasionally looking at each other.

She wasn't sure why Vince unsettled her the way he did. She never knew what to expect in terms of her emotions, and so she could never prepare herself for him.

"What are you after this morning?" Vince asked at last.

Her mouth twitched. "You really think I'm going to tell you?"

"So you do have something in mind you want?"

"Actually, not really. There's supposed to be some good stuff here but nothing I absolutely have to have, so my competitive instincts should be fairly reined in. I may not buy anything right now unless I find a great deal. I'll come back on the last day and see what's left that's been reduced in price. You should be safe right now from my competitive instincts."

He chuckled, his eyes resting on her face.

Her heart did a silly skipping thing in her chest.

"Did your mom send you here to get something?" she asked.

"You think I'm going to tell you if you won't tell me?"

"Just wondering."

"She actually didn't. She told me to go and grab anything that looks good and that isn't too expensive." He shook his head. "She has more faith in my ability to spot good antiques than I do."

"You seem to have done okay so far."

"You think so? Thanks. I've been studying my ass off, trying to get up to speed. But it's not something you can pick up overnight."

"No. It's not. But you seem to be doing fine."

She was surprised and strangely fluttery at the idea of his studying antiques so he could do a good job with his mom's store. She wasn't exactly sure why she was responding this way, but she couldn't deny it.

The most she could do was hide it from him since it would be very embarrassing if he found out she was feeling this way.

Another car pulled up, and a couple Liz was friendly with came up to get in line, so the conversation shifted with the newcomers.

Liz still felt like Vince was watching her sometimes, but she could never catch him doing it, so it might have just been her imagination.

~

Vince had no idea what he found so fascinating about Liz Berkley, but after six weeks it wasn't going away.

He was no longer annoyed by this response to her.

He was rattled.

Knocked off his feet.

He'd tried staying away from her, and he'd tried keeping her at a comfortable distance. Neither strategy worked. Even when he wasn't around her, his thoughts were filled with her.

So he'd been looking forward to seeing her at the estate sale this morning, and he hoped he hadn't come across as too much of a besotted idiot.

He didn't like to be this way—so out of control—but he wasn't sure what he could do about it except hold on to the last threads of the person he'd always believed himself to be.

Maybe if he could have sex with her, this obsession would finally pass.

She was attracted to him too. He was sure of it. She might not like him, but there was something fierce and carnal that radiated between them.

She might not be completely opposed to having sex with him either.

It was something to think about.

Liz wasn't as laser focused at this sale since there was evidently nothing here she was dead set on obtaining. So when the door finally opened and the first group was allowed into the house, she slanted him a playful look over her shoulder as she started toward the dining room.

"Tell me what you're heading for," he said, coming up beside her, "and I'll race you for it."

She laughed, the sound a small victory. "You're out of luck today. I'm just going to make a leisurely circuit and see what I see."

"Then you won't mind if I make the circuit with you. I don't want to miss out on a treasure."

"If there's a hidden treasure here, I'm going to grab it first."

They walked around the lower floor, and Liz stopped in front of several items but didn't claim anything. The furniture was all modern replicas of antique styles, and the paintings were evidently not valuable enough to tempt her. She lingered longer over a few pieces but didn't try to buy them, so they might be ones she'd look for later after the prices had lowered on the last day. Vince did try to look for himself, trying to think of what his mother might like to acquire, but nothing he saw seemed worth the trouble of buying and hauling home.

He asked Liz a couple of questions along the way, and she answered him without hesitation, even though she might have had a few qualms about educating the competition.

She obviously loved antiques and the whole business with a full-throated passion he wasn't sure he'd ever felt for anything.

The recognition hit him strangely. Made him feel odd.

After a while, he decided Liz might get annoyed if he trailed her the whole time, so he went off on his own to look around the upper floor.

He found a small mantle clock from the thirties that was dirt cheap, so he picked it up. The lines were good and the mechanism was original. It needed to be shined up and a few quick fixes, but once that was done, they'd be able to ask a lot of money for it.

Otherwise, he wandered aimlessly, and even though he tried to stay away from Liz, he somehow ended up in the bedroom where she was.

She was kneeling on the floor next to a small wooden box that had delicate flowers painted on the top. She was stroking the top of it.

"Find something good?" he asked, standing above her.

She gave a little jerk, as if she hadn't been aware of his presence. "Isn't it pretty?"

He knelt down beside her so he could see it better. There was a thick area rug beneath them, so they weren't kneeling on the hardwood floor. "Is it valuable?" he asked, intrigued by her reaction to the small, simple box.

"Is that always your first question?" Despite the words, her voice was light and not particularly sharp. "I asked if it was pretty."

"Oh. Yeah. Of course it's pretty. You like it?"

"Yeah." She turned to smile at him, her hand still resting on the lid of the box. "I love boxes and trunks and chests and jewelry boxes. Anything with a lid and space inside."

"Really? Why do you like them so much?"

"I don't know. I've just always loved them. You should have seen my room as a kid. It was filled with all these boxes—most of them totally worthless." She sighed and focused on the box again. "This one isn't really valuable. It's probably only about twenty years old, and the artwork is done by hand but not by anyone important. But I still love it. I might just buy it for myself."

"You should, if you like it that much. They're not asking that much for it."

"I know. I probably will." She looked at him again, her expression changing. "What did you find?"

He showed her the clock.

"That's a good find," she said, sounding completely sincere. "It needs some work, but nothing specialized. When it's cleaned up, someone will buy that for a good price."

"That's what I was hoping." He felt a ridiculous rush of pride and pleasure at her affirmation. The kind of response a boy would have to a pat on the head.

What the hell was wrong with him?

"I didn't see anything else," he said, trying to sound normal and not sure he succeeded.

"There's not much else here."

"No clothes at this one?"

"No. Well, there are plenty of clothes but just normal stuff. Nothing vintage or designer."

"No wedding dress?"

"No." A smile hovered on the corners of her lips like the most enticing secret. "Not this time."

"What did your folks think of that wedding dress?"

"Well. Uh…"

"You didn't give it to them?" He found this side of her fascinating and wanted desperately to know it more fully.

"No. I couldn't. I bought it with my own money and kept it."

"What did you do with it?"

"Right now it's hanging against a wall in my bedroom so I can look at it all the time." She laughed irrepressibly at herself. "I think Em must be rubbing off on me. Did you see that wedding dress hanging in the empty room of her place?"

"No! I must have missed it."

"Next time she invites you over, be sure to check it out. It's gorgeous, and it's the only thing in the room."

"I thought she wasn't planning to get married."

"She's not. But she wanted the wedding dress anyway. So maybe she was the one who inspired me about my own dress. I'll eventually have to put it up somewhere so it can stay in good condition. Or, if I feel too guilty about keeping a dress I don't need, I'll give it to the store and make a commission off it."

"Would you wear it to your own wedding?"

"I don't know. Maybe. It would need some alternations and… who knows?"

"Who knows what?"

"Who knows if I'll even get married?"

91

They were still kneeling together on the floor of the bedroom in the middle of an estate sale, and neither of them seemed aware of the inappropriateness of the location for a long conversation. "Is that something you want? To get married?"

She shrugged. "I don't know. Maybe. If I find the right guy. I'm not in a rush or anything, but I'm not set against it. Not everyone gets married. I'm sure it will be fine either way. I wanted the dress regardless."

"Yeah. I can see that."

Someone else came into the room just then, and it appeared to remind Liz of their location. With a self-conscious laugh, she pushed herself up to her feet, rubbing her back as if it were sore. She leaned down to put her hand on the box, clearly claiming it as hers as the man made a brief tour of the room and then left.

Then Liz stepped into the hall to call someone in to put a sticker on the box as a sign that it had been sold. "There's a basement here," she said. "I guess we should check it out, just to be sure there's nothing there."

"Sounds reasonable."

They headed down to the finished basement, but there wasn't much there—just some oversized furniture, basic electronics, and a lot of board games. Someone could stock a family room with the furnishings, but they were of no interest to antique hunters.

Liz shook her head, leaning against a wall around the corner from the stairs and staring out into the yard. "Pretty disappointing for an estate sale of this size."

"The listing was deceptive." Vince leaned against the wall beside her. "But I guess that's probably the way it goes."

"Yeah. Searching for antiques and collectibles is a lot of work and frustration and only the occasional thrill."

"Very encouraging. Thanks."

She chuckled. "Might as well get used to it now, if you're going to do this for any length of time."

"Yeah."

"Are you?"

"Am I what?" It was a genuine question. He'd been admiring the graceful curve of Liz's neck and the way it eased down into the swell of her breasts, and he'd momentarily lost track of their conversation.

"Planning to do this for any length of time."

He blinked, mentally catching up again. "Oh. Yeah. I don't know. For a while. As long as my mom needs me. So far, it's been better than I thought."

"Really?"

"Yeah." He was surprised to realize he meant it. Everything he'd thought would be frustrating about the move had gotten better as he adapted.

And the fact that he could see Liz so often made even the mundane more exciting.

"Have you found something yet that takes your breath away?" Liz asked, turning to face him more fully.

Vince froze, momentarily dazed. Had she somehow managed to read his mind?

"An antique or piece of art or something?" Liz added, bringing clarity to his unspoken question.

"Oh. No. I don't think so. Definitely not like you and the box or the dress."

"Well, you're never going to find something like that if you don't open up a little."

"Open up?" He was standing stiffly now, his chest tightening with either fear or anticipation.

"Open up. To feelings. Let go, like we were talking about with books. You know exactly what I'm talking about, so don't stare at me like I'm crazy or something."

"I'm not staring like you're crazy. I'm just not sure it's... me. To get exhilarated over a box or a dress."

"It doesn't have to be one of those things. Those are my things. What are *your* things? What exhilarates you that way? That's what you need to figure out, and then you need to... let yourself go a little or you'll never really embrace them."

Vince couldn't look away from her now, and his body was tightening with more than emotion. She might as well have been talking about herself.

Because *she* was what got his feelings in an uproar. *She* was what he wanted to look at every day, touch, caress, bury himself inside.

She was the only thing that had exhilarated him in a really long time.

Her cheeks flushed slightly and her eyelids dropped. "What?"

"What, what?"

"Why are you looking at me that way? It's not that strange to get excited about things, to really get into them."

"I don't think it's strange." His voice was huskier than normal, and he knew why. His pulse was throbbing in his throat, his wrists, his ears.

And now his groin.

"Then what?"

"You really don't know?"

Her eyes flew up, and he saw the moment that she recognized how he was feeling. "Oh."

"Oh," he repeated, turning slightly so his body was almost aligned with hers.

"What was it that turned you on? Searching for antiques or me lecturing you?" Her voice was tart, but she was deeply flushed now, and her chest was rising and falling quickly. She was feeling it too.

"Definitely your lecture." He tilted his head down, waiting to see if she'd pull away, push him back.

She didn't. "You're a very strange man."

"No argument here."

Then he kissed her—the way he'd wanted to since that first night at the party six weeks ago.

She made a sound in her throat and wrapped both arms around him, immediately hot and sweet and eager. His head roared, and his body throbbed as he leaned into her, feeling the soft curves and firm contours of her body against his. She moved her mouth against his until both his lips were cradling her upper one, and he couldn't keep his tongue still. He slid it against the crease between her lips until she opened for him. Then his tongue was all the way inside her mouth.

He was deep.

Arousal pulsed painfully at the front of his trousers, and he realized he was rubbing himself against her middle.

He was out of control. Completely.

If he could, he would take her right now, right here.

He wouldn't be able to stop.

It made no sense, and his need for it was as terrifying as it was exhilarating.

The fear was enough to distract him.

This wasn't staying on the surface. This wasn't keeping his life under control the way he always had before.

This wasn't taking the easy way—the way that wasn't going to hurt him.

Nothing about Liz would ever be easy.

Or safe.

He wanted this so much, but he wasn't sure the person who was feeling so deeply was... him.

At least not the him he'd always been.

He pulled back slightly, trying to catch his breath and clear his mind.

Liz panted and clung to him, her cheeks red and her eyes wild but a knowing smile on her full lips. "That's what I thought."

"What is?"

"That you're afraid to really let yourself go."

"What do you think I just did?"

"You let yourself go a little, but then you stopped yourself from going too far."

"You wanted to do more than kiss right here, right now?"

Liz laughed. She was obviously aroused too, but she was a lot more composed than he was. "No. That probably would have been a bad idea. But that's not really the point."

He was confused. Befuddled. He didn't know what was happening. "What's the point?"

"The point is that you just stopped yourself from letting go, the way you always do. There are no stakes here. Anything between us would just be physical, casual. Both of us know that. But you won't even fully let yourself go when there aren't any stakes. One day you're going to have to admit that your mom and I are right about you. And then what will you do?"

He stared at her, completely dumbfounded by her words, how far they pierced his heart. And he hadn't pulled himself together—not even close—when she was turning her back to him, walking away.

She was leaving him, as if what had just happened between them hadn't rocked her completely, the way it had him.

Maybe it hadn't.

She'd assumed there could never be anything serious between them. Nothing any deeper than their physical bodies.

Maybe he was in this thing a lot deeper than she was.

He couldn't let it remain that way.

SIX

When Liz got home a few hours later, Jane and Em were sitting on the terrace, drinking coffee and eating pastries Em had brought over. Anne was out of town on a business trip, or she probably would have been over there too.

Normally this would have been good news to Liz since she loved hanging out and eating tasty treats, but she was in an emotional flurry from the kiss with Vince, and she wasn't sure she'd be able to hide it from the others.

She wasn't sure why she even wanted to.

She wasn't in the habit of keeping secrets from Jane and Em.

Vince had gotten her all topsy-turvy.

"Come on out!" Em called, when Liz walked in and put down her bag and the painted wooden box she'd bought for herself at the sale. "I ordered from Stella's."

Stella's—a local bakery and sandwich shop—didn't usually make deliveries on Saturday mornings, but they made an exception for Em.

Everyone made exceptions for Em.

"I'll be there in a minute," Liz called back, going to the bathroom and then washing her face and hands in an attempt to refresh herself and cool down.

She stared at herself in the mirror, breathing deeply. Her cheeks were still flushed, and her eyes looked too wild. Waves of hair and flyaways were coming out of her ponytail.

Jane and Em were going to know something had happened.

They'd know as soon as they saw her.

She composed her face and went out to the terrace, hoping for the best.

"What in the world happened?" Em demanded, putting down the last bite of the chocolate croissant she'd been eating.

"Nothing. Just a lot of hassle at the sale." Liz was pleased with the casualness of her tone. She poured the remainder of the coffee in the french press into an empty mug, took an orange scone from the box in the middle of the table, and sat down next to her sister.

Both Jane and Em were staring at her fixedly.

"What?" she asked, giving blithe ignorance one more try.

They didn't answer. Just waited.

"Oh fine!" Liz rolled her eyes and then leaned over to peer at the next-door terrace. It looked like the french doors leading out to it from Vince and Charlie's unit were closed, but she wanted to make sure before she started talking.

"They're not home," Jane said quietly.

"Now tell us," Em added.

Liz rolled her eyes again before she announced, "I kissed Vince this morning."

The response to that claim was every bit as dramatic as she'd imagined. Em squealed and clapped her hands, and Jane gasped, covering her mouth with one hand.

"Tell us everything," Em said.

"I don't even know how it happened. He was at the estate sale early again, and we talked some, and then we looked around, and then we were in the basement, and then he was suddenly kissing me."

"So he kissed you first?" Jane asked.

"Yes. Of course. I never would have kissed him since I'm not even sure I like him. But I did... I guess I did kiss him back."

Em leaned forward. "And how was it?"

"It was... It was good."

"What did he say afterward?"

"I don't know. He pulled away after we'd... we'd kissed for a while. And I said something casual. And then I left."

"So he didn't say anything at all?" Jane's voice was gentler than Em's, but she looked just as invested in the questioning.

"Oh. Yeah. He did. He said something about how we couldn't do more than kissing where we were—which was obviously true."

"So it sounded like he wanted to do it again?" Em asked.

"I don't know. And the truth is I'm not sure it matters if he wants to do it again. I'm not sure I *want* him to do it again." She could see the question on Em's face, so she forestalled it with an answer. "It was good. A really good kiss. And I was as into it as he was. I know doing more would be... fun. But I have to really think through whether I'd want to just play around like that. I'm not against casual sex. I'd just have to be really sure I was fine with a casual thing before I did anything else." She hated admitting this last thing—even to herself—but she wasn't going to let herself fall into a situation where she wanted more from a relationship than Vince could give.

Jane reached over to pat her arm in a comforting gesture. "So you think all he wants is casual?"

"I have no idea what he wants, but I think right now he's only capable of being casual. He's pretty much admitted it to me. He doesn't go deep. And obviously I wouldn't want to go deep with him anyway. He's not my type, and I'm not sure I even like him. But I just don't want to get tangled up in a complicated mess, just because I find him so hot." She shifted in her seat, suddenly self-conscious about the admission. "If you know what I mean."

"Of course we know what you mean. And that sounds like a very wise and mature thing to do." There was a quiver in Em's voice, although her big hazel eyes were wide and sincere. "Don't let his hotness convince you to do something stupid."

"Unless you really want to," Jane added. "Maybe he wants to go deep too—for the first time."

"No. He's not going to do that. Guys don't change overnight, you know." Liz was feeling better now that she'd talked things through. Not quite so emotionally upended. "Hot sex is hot sex, and it could be exactly what I need. But I have to be sure it's what I really want. Anyway, he's the one who pulled back from it, so he might have just got caught up in the moment. He might not want anything more from me."

"Maybe you can leave it open," Jane put in. "Just to see what he wants to do. And what you want to do."

"There's nothing in the world wrong with having a little fun with a hot guy, as long as you're honest with each other," Em added.

"I know. I'll think about it and see what happens." She decided it was time to change the subject since she was feeling too exposed. Vulnerable. "Now tell me about you, Jane. How did things go with Charlie last night?"

Charlie had taken Jane to dinner and the grocery store last night. Another outing under the guise of being helpful.

"It was good."

"He still hasn't asked you out for real?" Liz asked.

Em shook her head. "That's what we were just talking about when you came in. He hasn't asked her out for real. He hasn't kissed her or anything."

"I'm starting to think he just wants to be friends." Jane's eyes were downcast, but her expression was composed. "Which is fine. I'm happy to have him as a friend."

"There's no reason to assume that. It's been only a couple of months since his breakup. He might just need more time," Em said. "He might want to take it slow."

"Or maybe he just wants to be friends." Jane shrugged. "I'm fine if that's what he wants."

"No, you're not. Maybe you should just kiss him," Em suggested.

"That's what I've been telling her," Liz said. "She needs to let him know for sure she's interested."

"It's not my way." Jane fiddled with her coffee cup.

"I know. But I've told you before. Guys tend to be wusses. Not many of them will pursue someone if they don't get a lot of encouragement."

"I say yes to everything he asks me!" Jane's voice was more vehement than normal. "How much more encouragement does he need?"

"He needs more," Em said, sounding dry and ironic and experienced, although she'd had no romantic relationships in her life that had lasted more than a month. "Guys always need more. And I'm telling you that you need to seal the deal with him soon. He's cute and nice and loaded. Girls are always chasing him down. You're not going to find a guy like him again—one you can get along with and whose family can bail your family out of your... financial issues. Don't let him get away."

"Don't make it sound so mercenary," Jane objected. "I'm not like that."

"Of course not." Em's hazel eyes sparkled with wry humor. Both Jane and Liz knew she was teasing and didn't actually think Jane was interested in Charlie for his family's money. "You're not after a guy for his money. You're just after a guy who happens to have it. Nothing wrong with that."

~

That evening, Vince was in a bad mood because he couldn't get Liz out of his mind.

Or his body.

He was on edge. Still pulsing with energy, interest, a low-level arousal. Like his body knew something needed to happen and it wasn't going to let him relax until it did.

He didn't like feeling that way. He didn't like feeling like a part of himself was out of control. It caused a knot to tighten in his gut. The one that reminded him of Georgie.

The one that sparked that lingering fear that things were getting too serious, too dangerous.

And it was worse because Liz didn't appear to be in the same emotional place.

It affected his mood.

He and Charlie were hanging out, watching a baseball game on TV and eating pizza, but Vince kept snapping at his friend.

He couldn't seem to stop himself.

After a couple of hours, Charlie finally said, "Damn it, man! If you want to be by yourself, just say so."

"I don't."

"Then what the hell is wrong with you?"

"Nothing. Just in a foul mood. Sorry."

"Is there any reason for your mood?"

Vince and Charlie weren't prone to having heart-to-hearts, so Charlie's question was mostly casual.

Vince shrugged it off. "Just one of those days. What about you? Anything happening with Jane?" The question was offhand, but it made Vince feel strange and awkward, especially after the snippet of a conversation he'd overheard from the women on the terrace as he was getting back home that morning. Maybe they'd been joking. Surely they'd been joking. Surely Jane wasn't going after Charlie for his money.

Some people did that, sure. But he hadn't thought Jane seemed the type.

He'd only heard a few sentences, and the voices had been muffled by the closed doors, so it was entirely possible he wasn't getting the full context.

He hoped so.

"Not really," Charlie said. "I'm hoping she likes me, but she's kind of hard to read. I've been taking it slow anyway—to make sure I'm over what happened with Melanie."

Vince felt another prickle of worry. "Taking it slow is smart. If you don't think she likes you in the same way you like her, then it might be smart to give her a little space."

Charlie frowned, his open face uncharacteristically glum. "You think she doesn't like me?"

"I don't know. But I've looked and I don't..." Vince decided to just say it. He'd already wondered if Charlie's interest might be one-sided, and the piece of conversation he'd overheard seemed to confirm it. "I don't see any clear signs of it. Usually women will let you know if they're interested, and she acts kind of standoffish."

Charlie slumped back against the couch, rubbing his face with both hands. "That's what I was afraid of. I'm so out of practice at this. Melanie was the only woman I've ever..."

His breakup with Melanie had hit him hard. Vince wasn't about to let his friend get into a new relationship that would hurt him even worse.

"I'm not saying give up. You can give it a little more time. But I don't want you to get hurt if she's... not in the same place you are. Maybe back off a bit and see if she makes a move to get closer. That might make it clear if she's really interested."

"Yeah."

Vince felt like shit when he saw his friend's expression, but he wasn't sure what else he could do.

If there was something he could do to help Charlie, he was going to do it. Even if it hurt.

He hadn't done enough to help Georgie, back when there might have been something he could have done.

He wasn't going to make that mistake again.

~

Later that night, Vince lay in his bed, trying to go to sleep. Trying not to think about Liz.

She'd said he couldn't let go, that he couldn't open up to real feelings.

She'd acted like he was incapable of it instead of it being his own choice.

He kept replaying the conversation in his head. All the conversations he'd ever had with her.

His body was hot and aroused, even as that knot tightened in his gut again.

He shouldn't be capable of feeling both of them at once.

He didn't want to feel both.

Lust was easy. He was used to it.

But all this other stuff complicated the hot rush of arousal.

Maybe she and his mother were right. He couldn't do anything deeper than the surface. He should just let it go and be the man he'd always been.

But he didn't want it.

He wanted more.

Bigger.

Stronger.

Deeper.

Why the hell shouldn't he try it?

He didn't like the idea that he wasn't capable of doing something he wanted to do.

He sat up straight in bed, breathing fast and hard and sweating just slightly.

Then he made his decision.

If it was nothing more than casual, then he could at least enjoy some hot sex.

And if it was more—if it *could* be more—he wanted to find out.

He jumped out of bed, threw on some clothes, left his condo, and walked one door over to bang on Liz's door.

~

Liz was getting ready for bed—putting a few stray dishes in the dishwasher and turning out the lights in the great room—when she heard the knock on the door.

It was after midnight.

No one should be coming over at this time.

Something must be wrong.

Her first thought was for Em. Maybe her father was sick or had fallen. She ran to the door quickly and flung it open.

Not Em.

Vince.

Standing in the hallway. Wearing nothing but a pair of black sleep pants. Bare chest. Bare feet. Rumpled hair. Five-o'clock shadow. Strangely urgent gray eyes.

"What are you—"

"You're wrong," he interrupted abruptly.

She blinked. "What?" Before he opened his mouth to talk again, she made a shushing gesture and glanced behind her to the stairs that led up to Jane's bedroom. "Keep your voice down. Jane is already asleep. Now what the hell has gotten into you?"

"You're wrong," he said again, stepping into the entryway when Liz moved out of the doorway.

"I'm not wrong." Her first response was automatic. A reflex. Then she frowned and added, "What am I wrong about?"

"About me. You're wrong about me."

They stared at each other in the dim light of the room for a moment that lasted far too long. Tension shuddered in the air between them. Liz's breathing quickened. Her skin warmed. She licked her lips self-consciously.

"I *can* let go. I can let go all the way." Vince seemed nothing at all like himself. He was wired. Urgent. As sexy as hell with his naked chest and barely reined intensity.

She was trapped by his gaze the way she'd been that morning. But this was even more. Even hotter. She suddenly made up her mind. She'd regret it all her life if she didn't give in to the force of the attraction she felt for Vince even if it was only casual sex.

She'd never wanted someone like this before. She might not ever feel this way again.

She didn't want to miss out on it forever.

"Then do it," she said, her voice barely a rasp. "Do it."

Vince stared at her for another few seconds. Then, without warning, he was kissing her hard.

It happened so quickly she wasn't prepared. She couldn't compose an appropriate response. All she could do was follow the demands of her body and heart.

Both of them—all of her—wanted to kiss Vince back.

So she did.

She grabbed for him, partly to keep her balance and partly so he wouldn't pull away like he had this morning. She opened her mouth and tried to suck his tongue toward hers, needing to feel him as deeply as she could.

He'd taken her head in both his hands to hold her face in place, but after a minute he slid one of them to her back and then lower to her bottom.

She thrilled with the feel of it. Of him. His mouth, tongue, hands, body. He was so hot she was afraid he might burn her, but it was a fire she wanted. She clawed at the skin of his back, her fingernails skimming over his shoulder blades, and she gave a huff of surprise and pleasure when he suddenly swung her up into his arms.

It was the last thing she expected, but the gesture did her in completely. She grabbed his head as he walked, kissing him with a passionate eagerness she'd never let herself feel for anything but antiques and books.

He carried her toward the stairs but stopped partway there. She broke out of the kiss and checked his face, realizing he didn't know where to go.

"The one at the end of the hall on this floor," she said with a giggle smothered in his mouth.

He grunted a wordless response as he completed his route to her room.

Liz kicked the door closed with her foot, wishing she'd picked up a little. There was some clean laundry draped over the chair in the corner and a couple of pairs of shoes in the middle of the floor. Jewelry spread out over her dresser.

The gorgeous wedding dress was still hanging on a hook on one wall. She still hadn't managed to put it away.

"This is casual, right?" she asked, pulling her mouth away from his. "Hot sex. No strings."

He blinked, like she'd surprised him. Or maybe he was just orienting his thoughts. "Oh. Yeah. That's okay with you, isn't it?"

"Yes. It's fine. I just want to make sure we're on the same page. If this is just a one-night stand, then maybe I should shove the wedding dress in the closet." She was pleased with the amused lilt to her voice. Maybe she was better at casual sex than she'd thought. "It might cast the wrong kind of mood."

He gave a low chuckle. "Do it." He carried her over to the dress, and she grabbed it from the hook and then hung it in the closet when Vince brought her close enough to do so.

Once that was taken care of, she could focus on what was most important.

Vince. Hot and sexy and raring to go. His eyes were devouring her face and body as he leaned over to place her on her bed. She reached up to pull him down on top of her.

He wasted no time in kissing her again, moving on top of her so he was straddling one of her legs and holding himself up on his forearms. Part of his weight was resting on top of her, and it was big and hard and smolderingly hot. She felt small beneath him, and she wasn't used to feeling that way.

For some reason it turned her on even more.

She'd wrapped one leg around him in an attempt to ease the ache at her center, and her squirming eventually managed to find the bulge of Vince's erection in his pants. He groaned into her mouth, his tongue growing still.

She ground herself against him, whimpering in pleasure.

"Oh fuck," he gasped, tearing his mouth away. "You're so hot. So… so…"

She loved the helplessness of his voice, like he was feeling too much to handle. She slid her hands down to his ass and squeezed. "So what?" she prompted.

"So eager."

She stiffened. "Eager?"

"What's wrong with eager?"

"It sounds undignified."

He chuckled and brushed a light kiss against her swollen lips. "You think anything about this is dignified?"

"Well, you can do better than *eager*."

"Enthusiastic?"

"Try again."

His eyes were warm with both amusement and arousal, and she loved the combination. "Passionate?"

"That will have to do." She managed to free her other leg and wrapped them both around his hips, squeezing him between them in a way that made him let out a broken moan. "You seem kind of eager too."

His mouth hovered just above hers. "Passionate," he corrected. "And, yes, I am."

Then he kissed her again, just as deeply as before, and she stopped being able to work out specific moves. They kissed and caressed and clawed at each other's pajamas until both of them were naked. Vince suckled her breasts until she was whimpering, and then he felt between her legs, finding her wet arousal and stroking her there until she came all around his fingers with a breathless cry.

Her body was relaxing with a hot rush of satisfaction when she finally opened her eyes to see that Vince was smiling down in a very particular way.

She frowned. "Don't gloat."

"I didn't say anything."

"You didn't have to say anything. I can read that expression. You're all proud of yourself for making me come."

"Would you rather I not make you come?"

"I'd rather you not gloat about it."

He was still smiling. He couldn't seem to stop. But he made a visible attempt to control his expression. "How's that?"

"Not too good. You'll have to keep working on appropriate humility." She was teasing, and he knew it. She pushed him off her gently so she could reach over into the drawer of her nightstand and grab a condom from the pack she kept there.

She offered it to him, and he took it without hesitation, tearing it open and rolling it on.

She liked the looks of his naked body. All of him. He was big all over, and she was excited again when he settled between her legs, propping himself up on his arms above her. "Is missionary all right with you, or would you prefer a different position?"

"This is good. This is perfect. Now get going."

He chuckled as he aligned himself at her entrance and started to edge in. "Always a competition with you."

"If it's a competition, then I've already won." Her voice caught on the last word as her body adjusted around the length and girth of him.

"What was that?" Vince teased, although his voice was as breathless as hers.

"I said I already won."

He eased back slowly and pushed in again, the slow thrust making Liz gasp and grab for the sheet beneath her. "What was that again?" he asked with another taunting smile. His skin was slightly flushed and damp with perspiration.

"I said I—" She couldn't hold back a moan when he took another long thrust. She arched up into it eagerly.

"You said what?"

"I said—" She was moving with him urgently now, her body stimulated in every way imaginable. "I said I—" She hung on to his shoulders as they built up their rhythm.

"You what?" His face was twisting in effort and pleasure, so it was clear he was just as carried away as she was.

But if he could sustain their unspoken challenge, then she could too.

"I... already... won!" she managed to choke out, riding him frantically from below as another orgasm built inside her.

"Is that... what you think?" He was grunting now in time with his rhythm. It was the sexiest sound.

"Yes. I already..." She clawed lines down his back as she arched up, the pleasure coiling down tightly just on the cusp of release. Then her whole body shook helplessly as the waves of climax overwhelmed her. "Oh God. Oh God! I won!"

Vince made the strangest sound. It was like a strangled laugh. Then he froze for a moment, all the tension contorting his features, before he came too with a loud exclamation that sounded like, "Fuck, yes."

They shook and squeezed each other for a long time until the spasms finally faded. They gasped in unison, still tangled up together.

Finally Liz felt Vince's body shaking in a different way.

She stiffened and frowned up at him when he raised his head from the crook of her neck. "Are you laughing?"

"No. Never." Despite his words, he was having trouble controlling his expression.

"Why are you laughing?"

"Do you always cry out 'I won' when you come?"

Liz blinked. Thought back. Realized that was exactly what she'd done. She giggled helplessly and gave him a light swat on the shoulder. "No! Of course not. I was just finishing my earlier sentence about already winning. I just got distracted briefly by the orgasm."

"Ah. Is that what happened?"

"Yes. That's exactly what happened."

"I see." He was still shuddering with silent amusement, and Liz couldn't resist his warm expression.

She pulled him down into a hug.

She was feeling so good. So relaxed. So completely sated. So close to him, their bodies wrapped up in each other and their laughter wafting together.

But they'd clearly discussed what this was. One night of sex. The culmination of the attraction that had always sparked between them. And, unless he said something different, there was no reason to assume they'd ever have sex again.

It was fine. Everything was fine. She could handle anything that happened.

She just wanted to know what he was thinking.

"That was fun," she said at last.

"Yeah. Definitely." His relaxed tone did nothing to clue her in to what was going on in his mind.

"You definitely proved you can let go in the bedroom," she said lightly. "At least one time."

However he replied was fine with her. It was fine. She just needed to know right now.

"Glad you realize it." He rolled off her with a groan, taking care with the condom and then sitting on the edge of the bed to deal with it.

She waited, but he didn't say anything else. She needed a little more information. She couldn't put herself together and make a plan to deal with it until she knew. "Is that it then?" she asked, reaching down to grab a soft throw blanket to cover up with. She didn't like to lounge around naked after the sex was over. "Or do you have more to prove to me later on?"

He gave a little jerk and turned his head sharply in her direction. "I'm happy to prove to you anything you think needs proving. Just say the word."

All right then.

They could have sex again. Nothing more. Nothing deeper. But if she wanted another round of great sex, he was evidently available.

That was all she wanted. This was Vince Darcy, after all. He always kept control of himself. He never let go too much. He obviously wanted to indulge their attraction, but he'd never offer anything else.

She didn't even want it.

Not with him anyway.

She slanted him a grin. "Sounds good to me. Anytime you feel like you want to prove you can let go again, you come right over and do it."

He smiled, a tension in his shoulders relaxing. "Sounds like a plan."

All right then. Things were clear now.

She'd evidently said the right thing to him.

She was still in control of this, so she could have a little fun if she wanted.

SEVEN

Two weeks later, Vince had Liz's back against the wall.

Literally.

She'd been reading in her favorite spot—the far corner of the Pemberley House estate where there were a couple of comfortable lounges in a sunny spot surrounded by trees. Almost no one ever went there except her, but Vince ran the perimeter of the property every day, and he'd happened to catch her there today.

She wasn't quite sure how it happened. He'd stopped to say hello, breathing hard and damp with perspiration from his exercise. She'd teased him about keeping his distance while he was sweaty like that.

He'd taken the words as a challenge.

So now she was hot and gasping and slightly sore, trapped against the old stone wall that ran the border of the estate, her legs wrapped around his waist and held up by the press of his body.

"Well," she managed to say, trying not to giggle in pure giddiness. "That was unexpected."

"It wasn't unexpected for me." Vince was just as warm and breathless as she was.

"What? You mean you found me on purpose to have sex?"

"No. I mean the minute I saw you reading here, I knew sex was going to happen."

"What if I said no?"

"Then I wouldn't have done anything, obviously." He pulled back with an almost wicked glint in his eyes. "But you haven't said no to me yet."

Liz hadn't said no to him. At all. For the past two weeks, they'd had sex every single day. They'd find each other in free moments and take advantage of whatever private spot was available. Both of them agreed to keep their fling quiet, so she hadn't told anyone else about it. Not even Jane.

It was a fun, hot secret, and it didn't matter if that was all it was.

She was having a really good time. She'd never met a man who was as much of a match to her intelligence and quick tongue as Vince.

She was pretty sure he was having a good time too.

"There's always a first time," she said tartly, wriggling slightly until Vince loosened his hold on her and eased her feet to the ground. She pulled down the little cotton dress she was wearing—hopelessly wrinkled now—and rubbed her back. "I'm starting to regret saying yes this time. Now I'm all hot, and I smell like your sweat, and I've got bruises on my butt and my shoulder blades."

He frowned. "I wasn't that rough."

"Not rough. Just enthusiastic. I think it's clear which of the two of us is more *eager*." She giggled at his expression and stretched out on one of the lounges to recover and enjoy the aftermath of her orgasm. "You even bring a condom with you when you take a run."

"I'm not a fool. I bring a condom everywhere these days. But you were pretty damn eager yourself," he said. "I'm surprised half the estate didn't hear us, the way you were screaming your head off in your ecstasy."

She sucked in an outraged breath and sat up straight. "I was not screaming my head off. Don't exaggerate."

"It's not much of an exaggeration. You were really into it." He was on her before she knew to expect it, pushing her backward until she was reclining and his face was just above hers. "There was definite screaming involved."

"Don't exaggerate," she repeated primly, pleased to maintain her composure when he was so close, so hot and heavy above her.

His hands were moving now, sliding up her thigh. She'd kept her panties on before—he'd simply pulled them aside to enter her, another discomfort that hadn't mattered much in the heat of the moment—so now he tucked his fingers beneath them until he was stroking her intimately.

"Vince, we just had sex. I don't need a repeat performance."

"It won't be a repeat performance. Just proving my point."

His hand had stopped at her words, so she gave him permission with a wry shake of her head. "Prove away. But don't be disappointed if it backfires."

It didn't backfire.

She wasn't sure how he did it. It seemed like he just kissed her a little and felt her up, but it was less than a minute until she was feeling urgent again.

He smiled against her skin. "I love how, after we have sex, you're all primed and ready so it takes no time to get you going again."

"I'm not... going."

That was a manifest lie. She was shamelessly trying to ride his hand.

He chuckled and gave her neck a little nip, causing her to gasp and dig her fingers into the back of his neck.

"Okay," she admitted. "I might be... going a little. But I'm not going to scream or anything."

"We'll see."

She tried to hold out. She really did. But he had some sort of magic fingers, and her body simply wouldn't cooperate with her will. In about thirty seconds, she was shuddering through a hard climax, crying out her pleasure into the open air.

And Vince was laughing silently as he stroked her through the last of the spasms, his face almost tender in its amused warmth as he gazed down at her.

"That wasn't a scream," she managed to say as soon as she found some breath.

"If you say so."

"It wasn't. It was a very ladylike sound of completion." She tried to keep a straight face but failed completely. She was giggling as Vince pulled her into a soft hug that ended their debate.

She was feeling very relaxed and maybe a little sappy. She knew her relationship with Vince was sex only, but it was hard not to like him a bit. In her current mood, she might have said something embarrassing, but she was saved by the buzzing of her phone.

A glance at the screen made her shake her head. "It's Riot. She says, 'I'm here. Where are you?' with a lot of exclamation points."

"What does she want?"

"God only knows. The girl is always getting into some sort of trouble. Last month she decided she wanted to become an expert in the antiques business, so she trailed around behind me to a bunch of places until she finally got bored and gave up."

"She's always trying to get my mom to let her help with important things like counting money and making purchases," Vince said, sounding like he'd found Liz's sister rather frustrating in the past. "Fortunately, my mom always refuses. If she really wanted to learn, it would be one thing, but it seems more like she wants the end result without the work it takes to actually learn."

"That's exactly what it is. She sees my job and wants it, just like she saw the trivia team's trip to New York in high school and wanted it, without ever trying to study up or practice. Hopefully, next month, she'll find someone else she wants to be like and leave me and your mom alone."

With another shake of her head, she pulled away from Vince's warm body—not as easy as it sounded—and stood up, stretching out her tension before she leaned down to grab her e-reader. "I guess I better go see what she wants."

"I'm heading back too, so I'll walk with you."

She couldn't have explained why, but she liked that he came with her. And she liked his easy company as they made their way down the trails through the gardens and lawns of the estate.

She waved at Ward Knightley, who was trimming some shrubs as they passed, and in a few minutes they'd reached the parking area and Liz saw Riot's little red car.

She hated that her parents had bought that car for Riot when she started college since she'd done nothing to deserve it and they really couldn't afford it.

"Liz, Liz, look what I have!" Riot called out now, jumping up and down with unnecessary enthusiasm. "Hi, Vince!"

Vince gave Riot a half-hearted wave and murmured, "That's my cue to leave. I'll see you soon."

Liz said goodbye, relieved he was leaving because Riot might be silly but she wasn't stupid, and she didn't want her sister to even begin to suspect there was something going on between the two of them.

"You're all wrinkled," Riot said as Liz approached.

"Yeah, I was reading on a lounge chair. It wasn't good for my dress."

That excuse seemed to satisfy Riot, who was focused on her own business anyway. "Look what I've got! You're going to be so impressed." She popped open her trunk to show Liz what she had.

Liz had no idea what to expect—maybe she'd bought out the shoe department at Macy's again. But what she saw in the trunk were antiques.

Four of them. Two lamps with stained-glass globes. A large ornate jewelry box. And a tiny footstool with a garishly upholstered top.

Liz blinked, trying to wrap her head around what she was looking at. "Where did these come from?"

"I found them! All on my own. Aren't they great? I'm sure they're worth a lot of money."

"Well, not a lot," Liz said, eyeing the pieces with a practiced eye. "But they're not bad. This lamp is good. Once it's cleaned up, someone would pay around a hundred dollars for it. The other lamp has been altered—it looks like a couple of times—so it would only fetch maybe twenty bucks if someone happened to like it. And the jewelry box." She lifted the lid to examine the inside. "It's a nice piece, but it's been damaged. The price of fixing it would take most of the profit, but you could probably get something for it. And that footstool... nah. No one is going to want that thing. But they're not bad overall. Did you grab these at a garage sale or something? If you paid a few dollars for them, then you did well."

Liz had purposefully taken her inspection of the pieces seriously because she wanted to validate her sister's efforts—no matter how ephemeral her interest in antiques was. She thought she'd been encouraging, so she was shocked by her sister's reaction.

"That's a lie!" Riot snapped, closing the trunk so hard that Liz's hand almost got caught by it. "You're just being mean because you don't want any competition."

"I am not," Liz began. "I'm telling you the truth—"

"Oh shut up!" And with that, Riot flounced into the front seat of her car and slammed the door.

Liz stood for a minute, trying to control her annoyance. When she was younger, she used to lose her temper with Riot's foolishness, and it had led to loud, passionate fights.

Since she didn't want that to happen, she sucked in her frustration and let Riot drive away without further interaction.

It was too bad.

Her conversation with Riot had completely wiped away her leisurely satisfaction from her time with Vince.

Em and Jane had been watching her in the parking lot from the terrace. She learned this when she came in through the front door and Em called out, asking what Riot had wanted.

Liz told them she'd be there in a minute, and then she went to the bathroom and tried to pull herself together, splashing water on her face and brushing some of the wrinkles out of her dress.

When she walked out to the terrace where Jane and Em were sitting in their normal positions, she felt more like herself.

"So what was all that with Riot?" Em asked.

"Why didn't she come up?"

"She was in a snit because she bought some stuff at a yard sale or somewhere and it wasn't as valuable as she was hoping. She told me I was lying to her and flounced off."

"Why would you have lied to her?" Jane asked in her quiet voice.

"I wouldn't. But she decided I thought she was now the competition and I didn't want her to win." Liz shook her head. "The whole thing is ridiculous. I can't wait until she moves off this antique kick and onto something new."

"But the something new might be worse," Jane said.

"It's kind of cute," Em put in. "She's trying to be you. She looks up to you."

"If she really looked up to me, she would listen to me. And if you find it so cute, you try taking her under your wing and see how you like it." Liz made a face at her friend, which just made Em laugh. "So are y'all just hanging out here tonight?"

"Probably. Dad isn't feeling good, so he wants me to stay close in case he needs me."

As far as Liz could tell, Em's father was never feeling good, but Em never complained about taking care of him.

Liz glanced over at Jane, but her sister had lowered her eyes demurely and didn't add anything to the conversation.

"Charlie didn't call or come over," Em said, answering the unspoken question.

"What's gotten into him?" Liz wondered out loud. "He was so obviously crazy about you, and lately he's…"

"He's backed off," Jane said quietly. "He obviously wasn't as interested as you thought."

"Yes, he was." Liz couldn't understand it at all, but for the past two weeks, Charlie hadn't stopped by or made excuses to see Jane the way he'd done all the time before. He was very friendly every time they saw him, but he'd only spent time with Jane one time this week.

The difference was marked.

And very upsetting to Liz since it was obviously so upsetting to Jane.

"It makes no sense. It was love at first sight for him. We weren't wrong about him."

"Some guys are like that. They get real excited for a while, but then they move on." Jane's voice didn't break, and Liz could see she'd been telling this exact thing to herself over and over again.

"I remember this guy in college," Em said. "We both showed up for the interest meeting at the college newspaper, and he decided he was in love with me then and there. You've never seen a guy so devoted. He barely left my side for weeks. I liked him okay, but it was all a bit too fast for me, so I kept slowing us down. But I was really considering a relationship with him. And then one morning I woke up and he'd fallen in love with someone else and was swooning all over her instead."

"What?" Liz leaned forward, genuinely interested. "He never said anything to you about it?"

"Nope. Not a word to me. Ever again." She shook her head, her shiny hair slipping out of the loose knot she'd clipped it up with. "His name was Andrew. Andrew the Asshole. He had this annoying blond hair that he would swoop over his forehead. I'll never forget him. Imagine treating a perfectly nice girl that way."

"Why didn't you ever tell me about him?"

"I don't know. I guess I kind of forgot about him by the time I came home for break. I never was into him that much. But I didn't deserve to be treated that way. He just enjoyed falling in love and didn't want an actual relationship. Some guys are like that."

"See," Jane said. "Maybe Charlie's like that too."

"But I don't think he is," Liz insisted. "He was with his old girlfriend for years, wasn't he?"

"Yeah, but maybe he's changed," Jane said. "We don't really know him."

"Yes, we do. And something is wrong with the whole situation. I think you need to ask Charlie about it to find out what's really going on."

"I'm not going up to a man and demanding why he doesn't like me anymore. Who on earth does that?"

"I would," Em said. "If it were me. But I don't care about romance, so it's not likely to ever happen to me."

"I might do it too," Liz admitted. "If something didn't make sense about the guy's behavior."

"Guys' behavior never makes sense." Jane shook her head and went on. "No. Don't keep arguing. If I have a good opportunity, I might try to hint around, but I'm not going to just go over and demand he tell me why he changed his mind. He never made any promises to me. He never kissed me. We never had sex. He never even asked me out on a real date. He doesn't owe me anything. If he doesn't want me anymore, then he's allowed."

Liz still didn't think they knew the whole story, but Jane was clearly about to cry, and she didn't want to make her feel any worse so she let the topic drop.

"So what's going on with you and Vince?" Em asked in a familiar teasing tone.

Liz stiffened. "What are you talking about?"

"We saw you and him walking together earlier."

Relaxing at that explanation, Liz said casually, "He was running, and I was reading, and we happened to run into each other."

"Is he still as obnoxious as ever?"

"I guess he's not quite as bad as I thought at first, if you can get over the arrogance."

Both Jane and Em laughed, and Liz felt a little stab of guilt at keeping her relationship with Vince from them. But if she talked about it, it would start to become important to her.

So far she'd managed to keep it in perspective.

She wasn't going to mess it all up now.

~

That night, Vince was lying in bed, trying to go to sleep.

The room felt hot, even though he'd opened two of the windows and turned on the fan. His bed didn't feel comfortable. He kept tossing and turning.

And thinking about Liz.

The problem with a no-strings-attached affair was that you couldn't spend as much time with the other person as you might want. Having sex with Liz was better than anything, but it wasn't feeling like enough.

He wanted to see her more. Hang out with her more. Maybe even the spend the night with her.

She was just next door.

It was ridiculous that they had to act like virtual strangers while anyone else was around.

He lay and stewed about it for a long time until he finally couldn't stand it anymore. He reached for his phone and tapped out a text message to her.

You awake?

It was a full minute before she replied. *Now I am.*

Can I come over?

Right now?

Yes. Now.

Another pause. Then her answer came through. *Come on over. Just be quiet.*

He was grinning as he got up, ran a hand through his hair to smooth it down, and then hurried through the condo and down the hall to Liz's door.

He didn't have to knock since she'd already opened the door.

After she locked up again, they went into her bedroom and closed the door. Since they'd had sex that afternoon, Vince had more control than usual, so he was able to make it last a long time, spending a long time on foreplay and sustaining intercourse until Liz came and then came again.

He felt a lot better afterward as he held Liz in his arms. Her bed was a lot more comfortable than his was, so he decided to doze for a while with her instead of going right back to his own place.

She didn't object to this plan. Of course she was half-asleep, so maybe she didn't think it through.

Either way, Vince got to go to sleep with Liz that night after all.

~

He woke up several hours later, but it was still dark in the room. A glance at the clock proved it was just after four in the morning.

He'd gotten what he wanted. He'd gone to sleep with her. Now was the time to slip out of bed and sneak back to his own place before anyone saw him in her room and realized what they'd been doing.

But Liz was still sleeping, and he didn't want to leave her without a word.

That would be rude.

He rolled over, stretching his slightly sore muscles. His eyes had adjusted to the room so he could see Liz on the pillow beside him. She was lying on her side, her arms bent up against her chest in a tight huddle. Her thick hair was falling all over her shoulders and back, as well as spilling all over the pillow.

She looked lovely but different than normal—since her expression was so peaceful and unrevealing, so unlike her normal vivid intelligence and strong spirit.

She almost looked vulnerable.

Like she wasn't as untouchable as she always liked to convey.

Like she could be hurt.

The thought lodged in his chest and got in the way of his breathing. He wasn't used to thinking about Liz that way, and he wasn't sure what to do with the feeling.

He hadn't felt protective about anyone since his sister, and Liz wasn't anything like Georgie.

He shouldn't be feeling the urge to take care of her.

Before he could work out the emotion to his satisfaction, Liz shifted in bed until her eyes fluttered open. It took her a minute to orient herself. He could see the succession of expressions on her face.

"Why are you still here?" she finally asked groggily.

"Why shouldn't I be?"

"I thought you'd have left."

"I meant to. I fell asleep."

"Oh. I didn't think you did things like that."

"What things?"

"Falling asleep when you didn't mean to."

"Well, I do."

She was smiling now—the sweetest, sleepy smile. "Oh. I do too. Sometimes."

"I appreciate the qualification." Unable to resist, he pulled her toward him so her soft curves were pressed up against him.

"For God's sake, Vince, are you turned on again? Exactly how horny are you?"

"*Horny*? That's even less dignified than *eager*."

She giggled and pressed a kiss against the side of his jaw. "Sometimes the undignified word is the best one."

He kissed her then. Slow. Leisurely. Then, far before he was ready, Liz rolled away, settling on her stomach beside him. "I'm going back to sleep now."

He gave a huff of indignation even though he knew she was teasing him.

When she giggled again, he realized he'd let her score a win, so he thought quickly until he landed on a suitable response.

"Okay," he murmured. "You go right to sleep. I'll find some way to amuse myself."

She made a little move of her head, like she was about to turn to see his expression, but she stopped herself and seemed to purposefully relax.

He knew a challenge when he saw one. He adjusted so he could easily reach her, and then he started to stroke her body under the covers. She was wearing nothing but a slinky little gown, so he could feel every inch of her. Firm flesh. Lush curves. Fit muscles. Deliciously soft dips and clefts.

He took his time as his hand slid down her back to her ass and then lower to her thighs, playing with each tantalizing spot he could find.

Liz was responding. He could tell by the tightening of her muscles, the way she was shifting restlessly. And he knew it for sure when she let out a long, erotic moan.

Wanting to please her as much as he could, he nudged her hips. "Lift up for me."

She did as he said, raising her hips up off the mattress so her round little butt was in the air. The covers had slipped down, so he could see her fully, and the sexy position made his already pulsing groin harden all the way.

In this position, he could reach her easily. She was warm and soft and slick with arousal, so his fingers slid in easily. He pumped them, occasionally rubbing her clit, until she came, smothering her cry of release in the pillow, her inner muscles fluttering hard around his fingers.

Then he couldn't hold back any longer. He rose to his knees, fumbled with a condom until he'd managed to roll it on, and then entered her from behind, riding her hard and fast. Their labored breath was the only sound in the room, other than the shaking of the bed. He was filled with need and pleasure and a strange sort of dominance as he felt her coming again, just before he did.

Release took him hard. Stole his breath. Filled his head with a rush of something far more than physical pleasure.

Like he needed this—her—as much as he needed the air in his lungs.

He'd never felt anything like it, and it was clamped down into a familiar, heavy knot in his gut. The one that warned him things were getting too deep.

That he might drown in it.

Part of him wanted to drown if it meant he could stay in Liz's body, in her arms, in her bed, in her life.

Maybe drowning wouldn't be so bad.

～

An hour later, a faint edge of dawn was coming in through the windows, so Vince knew it was time for him to leave and go back to his own place.

He still didn't want to.

He was in a groggy, sated condition, tangled up with Liz under the covers, and she must have felt similarly because she was awake but hadn't kicked him out of her bed yet.

"I think it's really morning now," she said after a while. She'd turned over onto her other side so he was spooning her from behind.

"I'll get going as soon as I can move."

"Okay." She sighed deeply as he idly stroked her belly.

He was looking around the room at all her pretty possessions. Clothes, accessories, artwork, flowers, and so many kinds of wooden boxes. The room looked like her. Rich and vibrant and full of character and lovely and deliciously warm. "You sure do have a lot of boxes."

She giggled and swatted at his hand. "I told you I love them. I might have a small problem with being unable to stop buying them. There's a bunch more in the closet."

He chuckled. "If I gave you a shoe box, would you treasure that one too?"

"Of course not. The boxes have to be wooden, and they have to be painted. Don't ask me why. I don't make the rules."

"Which one is your favorite?"

She thought for a minute in silence. "My favorite is one I don't even own."

"Really? Who does?"

"This old fellow in town. Howard Edwards. He's about ninety years old, and he has all kinds of amazing antiques. He's got this hundred-year-old tabletop chest with the most amazing watercolors of birds and butterflies on the top. I remember seeing it as a girl, when my dad was visiting him, and thinking it was the most amazing thing that had ever been created. I still go by to see it sometimes."

"Why don't you ask him if you could buy it?"

"I've asked him before, but he won't give it up. He keeps saying he'll sell his best antiques before he dies so his distant relatives won't fight over them. When he does, I don't care how much money he wants for it, I'm going to buy that chest. Em said she'd lend me the money since there's no way my family could afford it. But I have to have it. I love it so much."

He squeezed her in his arms, not sure what to say because his heart felt so full. That knot was still there in his stomach, but it didn't feel so uncomfortable right now. It kind of matched the weight in his chest. Like he was full.

Like she was filling him.

"Maybe you'll get it someday," he said at last.

"I hope so. I'll be heartbroken if I don't." She seemed to realize how earnest she was being because she turned over with a teasing smile. "Now. You've lounged around being lazy long enough. You need to get out of here and back to your place before anyone wakes up and finds you here."

Her words were light, but they were a real dismissal. He could hardly blame her. He was the one who had invited himself over last night, and he was the one who'd refused to leave when he should have.

Now was the time.

Liz wasn't his girlfriend.

They were just having a casual fling.

And it wasn't her fault that he was starting to wonder whether things would be better if they weren't so casual.

Maybe being serious, going deep, wasn't as impossible as he'd always believed.

EIGHT

Two weeks later, Vince was working at the computer in the office of his mother's store with a deep sense of accomplishment. It had been a long, tedious process, but he'd just about finished getting the accounts ready for taxes.

He was praying they didn't get audited for any of the previous years. He was sure his parents had paid far more in taxes than they needed to—they were the kind of people who threw money at a process so they wouldn't have to go through a lot of hassle—but he shuddered at getting the paperwork ready for an audit process.

But last year's was in good shape now, and he'd set up a better system so the tax process in future years would go a lot smoother.

Once that was done, he'd have a lot more time on his hands. He could work more on the acquisition process and study up more on antiques and collectibles.

It was different than what he was used to, but it was kind of fun. And it was nice not to be tied to a desk and computer the way he'd been at his job before.

As surprising as it was to admit, he wasn't missing his life back in Blacksburg much at all.

At all.

"How's it going?" his mother asked as she came into the office with her hands full of clothes.

"Good. I've almost got this done. I'll go over it with you when you have time."

"Oh my goodness, no, sweetie. You know about all that money stuff. I don't."

"But don't you want to know—"

"You could explain it to me ten times, and I still wouldn't understand any of it. I trust you, and I never pay attention to all the money stuff."

"Okay. Whatever you prefer. But you might need to cool it a bit with the purchases. They've been getting kind of high in the past few months."

His mother frowned with a characteristically absentminded look. "Really? I didn't know that."

"I just noticed the credit cards were higher than they used to be." He'd assumed that his dad had reined in his mom's impulses before he died since the purchases had increased significantly in the past three months. "It's no big deal. But we don't want to spend all our profits."

"Of course we don't. I'll be good. I promise. But I did make some major purchases this week. I've been trying to get Mr. Edwards to sell his best pieces for years now, and he finally agreed. But we'll be able to turn them around right away. I've already got some buyers interested. So I don't think you'll have to lecture me about them."

"I'm sure that's fine then."

"You won't mind taking Fred and Will to go pick up the pieces tomorrow, will you? I want to close the deal before he changes his mind."

"That's no problem at all. What are you doing with all those clothes?"

"Oh. They need to be retagged."

"I thought Riot was supposed to do that."

"She was, but she got busy."

"Busy doing what? Playing on her phone?" He shook his head, trying to hold back his first instinct, which was to demand why Riot was still employed. "Don't go and do that for her. When she comes in again, make sure she does it. She needs to do the things you ask her to if she's going to work for us."

"Your dad always handled the management stuff. Can't you do it?"

Vince felt awkward about supervising Riot, given his relationship with Liz, but he could hardly use that as an excuse because neither his mother nor Riot knew about it.

No one was supposed to know about it.

That fact was starting to grate on him.

"Sure, I'll do it if you need me to, but I think we both need to work together, or she'll try to bypass me by going to you."

"Okay. You're right. I'll be tougher. I promise."

"Good." Vince was silently thinking that, if Riot was made to do a real day's work when she came in, she would get tired of the job and quit to do something easier.

He could hope anyway.

His mom walked over to put a hand on his shoulder. "It's good to see you like this."

He blinked. "Like what? Tired and grumpy and with a coffee stain on my shirt?"

"Yes. Exactly that." She laughed and ruffled his hair in a way that only a mother could do. "Taking care of people again. You're almost happy."

"I've always been happy."

"No, you haven't. You weren't happy at all for a long time. But lately you've been getting there, and it does my heart good to see it."

He opened his mouth to reply but didn't know what to say. He felt like squirming, which was a ridiculous impulse.

"So if there's something in particular that's been making you happy, maybe you could think about taking whatever steps are necessary to keep it."

He frowned up at her, although he knew exactly what she was talking about. "There's nothing—"

"Okay, okay. I'm not saying there is. I'm just saying you'll be a bigger fool than I know you to be if you let something that makes you happy slip away because you're too scared to make it yours for real."

Before he could shape a suitable response to that, she walked out of the office.

~

The following night, Liz did something very stupid and fell asleep in Vince's bed.

She shouldn't have even been in his bed, but he'd texted her at about ten the night before and said that Charlie was out for the evening and his bed was available if she was interested.

She *was* interested. She hadn't seen Vince all day and had been feeling the loss. So she'd snuck over, thinking an hour of sex would sustain her without anyone being the wiser.

But she'd fallen asleep afterward and didn't wake up until seven the following morning.

It was Saturday, and the only thing on her schedule was to give the local flea market a quick once-over, so it wasn't like she was late for anything. The problem was that this late in the morning, there was a reasonable chance that Jane was already up.

Or, even worse, Em, who often came over for coffee and pastries on the weekends.

She sat up abruptly, trying to get her bearings and think through what she should do.

Vince had been asleep, but at her move, he mumbled out a wordless reproach and pulled her back down so he was spooning her from behind again.

He seemed to like that position.

So did she.

His big, warm body cradling her always made her feel small and protected. Like she didn't have to always be completely in control.

So she didn't resist the move the way she should have. In fact, she snuggled back into him, trying to make her mind work clearly.

"It's late," she said.

"Not that late. Charlie doesn't get up until eight or nine on Saturdays." He sounded more awake now, but his voice was husky and relaxed. Deliciously textured.

"But Jane does."

"So?"

"*So?* You're asking me *so?* If Jane's up, I'm going to have a hell of a time getting in without her seeing me, and then she'll demand to know where I've been."

"Just don't tell her."

"I have to tell her something."

"Why?"

"Because she's my sister. You can't just tell your sister nothing."

"Why not?"

"*Why not?* You've obviously never had a sister, or you wouldn't ask that ridiculous question." Her voice was light, playful, in keeping with their normal banter and the current conversation. But she felt Vince's body change behind her at her last words.

She rolled over immediately so she could see his face. He felt tense, and his face looked shuttered. "Vince, what's the matter?"

He gave her a little smile. "Nothing."

"Don't give me that. Something's wrong. What did I say?" She was so worried she lifted a hand to cup his jaw tenderly. "Tell me."

He let out a breath and shook his head. "It's really nothing. Not your fault at all. But I do have a sister." He cleared his throat. "I did."

She couldn't hide her surprise. "What? I thought you just had the one brother."

"I had a sister. Three years younger than me. She died when I was a senior in college."

"Oh my God! I'm so sorry. What happened?" She didn't think through the wisdom of such a question. In their relationship, she probably shouldn't pry into his history and private griefs, but she was too overwhelmed to guard her words.

"Her boyfriend was… an asshole. He was drunk one evening as he drove her back to the dorms. They didn't make it."

"Oh my God. Oh my God!" She raised her other hand so she was framing his face with them. "Vince, I didn't know."

"I know you didn't. I never told you, and you've never known my family. I'm just explaining why I responded the way I did when you said I never had a sister."

"It was a terrible thing to say."

"Not if you didn't know. And you didn't." He leaned forward and kissed her gently.

She stroked his hair, his bristly jaw. "What was her name?"

"We called her Georgie. She was eighteen when she died. She was sweet and always happy. So nothing at all like me." He gave her a wry, slightly bittersweet smile. "We were both going to UVA. I was a senior. I was supposed to look after her."

"Oh no, Vince, please don't tell me you blame yourself."

"I don't. Not really. Not rationally. I did try to get her away from that guy. I knew he was bad news from the beginning. But she was eighteen, and she was crazy about him. She wouldn't listen to me." He let out a long breath, his body softening and his face more vulnerable than she'd ever seen it. "I still miss her."

"Of course you do." She readjusted so she could hug him tight. "I can't even imagine how it would feel to lose a sister that way. I'm so sorry."

He hugged her back. "Thank you."

After a few minutes, she murmured, "I bet you were a good brother."

"I tried." His voice was slightly hoarse. "I could have been better, but I tried."

"She knew you loved her."

"I think she did. I really think she did."

"I know she did." She pulled back so she could see his face, and the look there took her breath away. She kissed him because she couldn't rein in the power of what she was feeling.

He kissed her back immediately, deepening it with his lips and his tongue. When he eased her over onto her back and moved over her, he was obviously ready for more. She mumbled against his mouth, "What about morning breath?"

"What's morning breath?" He was pushing up the T-shirt—one she'd borrowed from him to sleep in—and was running his hands up and down her body.

She chuckled and buried her fingers in his thick hair. The truth was she didn't care much about morning breath at the moment. There was nothing even remotely unpleasant about Vince right now, about what they were doing. It was real and natural and as intense as anything she'd ever experienced. She hoped he felt the same way.

They kissed for a long time—slow and deep and tender—and she wasn't aware of any particular moment when it changed from kissing to sex. It was all part of one delicious tangle of emotion and physicality.

Before she sorted out specific moves, Vince was moving inside her, their bodies rocking together as they kissed, his tongue moving with the rhythm of his hips. Everything felt good. Too good. Better than she could begin to understand. She couldn't focus enough to work up toward a real orgasm, but she was gasping out in pleasure as they rocked, as they kissed.

Vince didn't have his normal control. He was grunting in his throat, even as their mouths moved together, and his release seemed to take him by surprise. He let out a sharp exclamation as he tore his mouth away from hers, his face contorted with pleasure.

He came inside her. She felt the spasms of his release, his body jerking against hers.

They hadn't used a condom—hadn't even thought about it—and she was wet between her legs as he started to soften above her.

She didn't even regret it.

Nothing had ever felt so good in her life. So real. So deep. So intimate.

Vince lifted his head, his expression finally looking more like himself. He gave her a little twist of a smile. "Sorry about the condom."

"That's okay. We weren't thinking. I'm on birth control, so unless you've got something going on in the health department that you haven't told me, we'll be fine."

"I'm healthy."

"Good. Me too. We should be fine."

They gazed at each other for a minute, and she was suddenly conscious of what had just happened between them, what she'd just been feeling.

It was wrong.

It wasn't what they'd agreed to.

It wasn't what she was supposed to feel.

Things were getting out of control, and she couldn't let them. She'd always been better and smarter than that.

Fighting the flicker of terror, she gave him a quick smile. "I really need to be getting back home now."

"Yeah. I guess so." Vince's face twisted briefly. "Liz?"

She'd been climbing out of bed, but she paused at his hoarse question. "Yes?"

His features tightened again. It looked like he was trying to say something, but she had no idea what it was.

Hopefully he wasn't going to tell her that things were getting too intense between them and they needed to call it quits.

That would probably be the smartest thing, but she didn't want to hear it.

Then Vince's face relaxed. "Let me check to make sure Charlie's not up and the coast is clear before you leave the room."

"Oh. Yeah. Good plan."

~

If Liz was hoping that her place would be as empty and quiet as Vince's had been when she came home, she was doomed to disappointment.

Jane was awake, sitting on the burgundy Queen Anne chair in their living room and staring down at her phone when Liz walked through the front door.

Jane glanced up when Liz entered. "I thought you were still in bed. Where have you been?"

"Out." It was a stupid answer, and Liz had no doubts that Jane would follow up and demand to know more details.

In some ways, it would be a relief to finally tell her the truth.

But Jane didn't ask any further questions or insist on a real answer. She looked back down at her phone.

This was sign enough that something was seriously wrong.

Liz immediately forgot about her own situation and flurry of feelings for Vince and hurried over to the chair next to Jane. "What's the matter?"

"Nothing." Jane didn't raise her head this time. Her face was hidden behind her loose hair.

"Jane, stop hiding right now. Tell me what's the matter."

Jane took a deep, purposeful breath and straightened her spine and her shoulders. She met Liz's eyes directly. "It's nothing important. Charlie went out on a date last night. A real date."

Liz's stomach twisted painfully. "With who?"

"I don't know."

"Then how do you know he had a date?" Liz had no reason not to believe the news. Charlie had been out late last night when she'd snuck into Vince's room.

"Em just texted to tell me. She's getting more information."

"Oh my God. I'm so sorry, Jane." She reached out to squeeze Jane's knee. She would have given her a hug, but her sister wasn't much of a hugger and Liz had always respected that.

"It's fine."

"No, it's not."

"Yes, it is. Charlie never really asked me out. We weren't going out or together or anything. He has every right to date who he wants. I was silly for hoping for anything with him."

"You were not silly. He gave you every sign he was crazy about you. I'm sure he was. We all thought he was waiting until he was ready for another serious relationship, and I'm convinced that's what was happening. I just don't understand what went wrong. Why didn't he ever make a move on you and get serious? He so obviously wanted to, and I just can't believe he's the kind of guy who'd play around with a girl's feelings that way."

"Maybe he decided I wasn't his type after all. It doesn't matter. It's over now, and he didn't do anything wrong."

Liz scowled. "We'll have to disagree on that." She picked up her phone and texted out a message to Em, asking if she'd found out anything.

Jane might want to let the whole thing drop, but Liz wasn't ready to do that yet.

Something was wrong. Very wrong.

She knew it.

Her phone buzzed, and she glanced down to see that Em had replied. *On way.*

"Em is coming over. Maybe she has some news."

Jane gave her a sad smile and didn't respond.

"If anyone can get to the bottom of it, Em can." Liz waited, phone in hand, until she heard a knock on the door. She ran over to let Em inside.

Em was wearing red silky pajama pants, a thick velvety bathrobe, and matching fuzzy slippers. Her hair was clipped up on her head. She ran over to sit down next to Jane, taking the seat Liz had been in earlier.

Liz pulled up a leather ottoman and sat on that. "So what did you find out?"

"I've made six calls this morning to get information, and I've got some news. None of it good."

Jane took a shaky breath. "Well, tell us what it is. I'm ready."

"It's not just bad news for you." Em slanted a look over at Liz. "Anyway, I'll start from the beginning. Charlie's date was with another teacher in his school. They went to a big banquet together."

"Oh," Liz said, blinking in surprise. "That doesn't sound too bad. Maybe it was just a friendly work thing."

"I don't know. Maybe. But from what I've heard he *has* moved on from Jane, and evidently it's Vince's fault."

This was so far from what Liz could have expected that she jerked visibly. "What?"

"All I can say is that I'm glad you didn't decide you were interested in Vince and that kiss stopped when it did because he's evidently a bigger asshole than we knew. He talked Charlie into dating this new girl and dropping Jane."

"*What?* No. I don't believe he'd do that." Liz could barely breathe over the sudden ache in her throat. Her vision was blurry, and she was clenching her hands at her side.

"I'm surprised you're defending him since you're the one who knew he was a jerk from the beginning. But, yes, he did. I got it from three different people who are friends of Charlie. It's got to be true. It was Vince. And what's worse is that he somehow convinced Charlie that Jane was only spending time with him because of his family's money. Like Jane was some sort of fortune hunter."

Jane met Liz's eyes, and Liz fought a wave of nausea at the surprise and grief in her sister's eyes.

How could Vince do something like that?

Why would he do it?

Surely he wasn't some kind of cartoon villain who hurt people just to hurt them, but she couldn't think of a single reasonable explanation for Vince telling Charlie something so manifestly absurd.

"All I can say is that Charlie needs to grow a backbone if he lets his buddy talk him out of dating the girl he wants," Em said, her expression tightening angrily. "But Vince had no business interfering in something that wasn't

146

his business at all. He's way more of an asshole than we realized. This isn't all he's done."

Liz felt sick. She'd just been in bed with Vince not twenty minutes ago, tangled up in his body, as close as two people could get. She covered her stomach with one hand and rasped, "What else has he done?"

"This part is what I meant when I said it's not just bad news for Jane. While I was talking to Melissa Turner about Charlie, she mentioned something else about Vince. You know she works for old Mr. Edwards."

"Howard Edwards?" Liz said. "Yes, I knew Melissa was one of his sitters." She was seriously about to be sick.

Howard Edwards was the old man who owned the beloved wooden tabletop chest she wanted so much. She'd told Vince all about it a couple of weeks ago and how she wanted it more than anything.

The conversation had meant so much to her.

It had been intimate. Special.

"Well, evidently Mr. Edwards sold a bunch of stuff to the Darcys."

For a moment Liz was slammed with heat, and she was absolutely convinced she was going to throw up. "Not my chest."

Em nodded, looking both outraged and sympathetic. "Yes. The chest. The chest and several of his other best antiques. He sold them to the Darcys. I checked with two other people to make sure I got the whole story, and it's definitely what happened. Vince came with a couple of their guys to pick them up yesterday afternoon. I don't understand how he even knew about Mr. Edwards's antiques or how he swooped in like that and talked him out of them, but he did."

Liz opened her mouth and tried to speak. Couldn't.

Vince knew because she'd told him about them. She'd stupidly, naively spilled all her feelings about them to him.

And evidently he'd taken advantage of her sappy stupidity.

She couldn't believe it.

She simply couldn't believe it.

But Em had confirmed it with multiple people. It had to be true. And, if Vince had been there to pick them up, he had to have known.

At the very least, he could have given her a heads-up in bed last night instead of taking sex from her after betraying her the way he had.

Any decent human being would have at least mentioned it to her.

Despite everything she'd just heard, she had a sudden flicker of hope. Maybe he'd bought the tabletop chest for her, as some sort of romantic gift. Because he knew she loved it so much.

But it couldn't be.

He would have given it to her when he saw her last night, or at least told her about it.

And he wouldn't have ruined Jane's happiness if he'd cared about Liz in any way. He wouldn't have assumed Jane was a fortune hunter.

No. There was no good explanation for this.

Vince was nothing but an asshole after all.

"Are you okay?" Jane asked, real concern in her voice.

"Yes," Liz managed to answer.

Em's eyes were worried. "You look like you're going to pass out. I know you really loved that chest. I'm so sorry to bring bad news, but I thought you should know right away."

With a massive effort, Liz managed to stuff her grief and rage down into a little ball at the back of her mind. "You were right. I needed to know. I am upset about it. I'd actually been thinking Vince wasn't so bad. But this leaves no doubt." She blew out a deep breath. "Okay. Nothing to do about it. At least not about the chest. But maybe we can still talk to Charlie. If this was Vince's doing, maybe—"

"No!" Jane interrupted sharply. "If he could be talked out of being interested in me so easily, then I don't want him. Don't do anything."

"Okay. I won't." Liz felt like a volcano on the verge of eruption. Like there was too much inside her to hold on to and soon it would all just burst out.

She couldn't let that happen around her friends. "I'm going to run take a shower, if you're all right. We can hang out together today and cheer each other up."

"Sounds good," Jane said with a little smile.

"I'll hang out with y'all too. And if I catch a glimpse of Vince, I'm really going to let him have it." Em snarled viciously. "Bastard."

Liz left before she burst into tears.

~

She cried in the shower for a few minutes, but it didn't help to relieve her feelings.

She wasn't the kind of person who suffered in silence. Who could hold back this kind of wave of resentment. She had some things to say. A lot of things to say.

She had to say them.

She wasn't going to let Vince beat her.

She wasn't going to let him win.

So, when she got out of the shower, she pulled her wet hair into a long braid, yanked on leggings and a clean top, and then stuffed her feet into slippers.

She looked terrible, but she didn't care.

She was going to tell Vince exactly what she thought of him.

Before she could get scared or talk herself out of it, she ran for the front door, calling out, "I'll be right back!"

She made a beeline for Vince's front door, but before she had even reached it, the door flew open and Vince stood in front of her, dressed in nothing but his sleep pants.

She blinked in surprise, momentarily distracted from the tirade that had been building up.

"Oh," Vince said, his face softening when he saw her. "I was just about to look for you."

"You were?" Her voice cracked. She needed a moment to recover her momentum.

"Yes. I had some things to tell you, and I was too scared to tell you before. But I need to do it. I need to do it right now."

He had some things to tell her. Things he was scared to admit. She could well imagine what they would be.

She opened her mouth to snap out a reply that anything he needed to say was unnecessary, but he beat her to it, words spilling out from him in an urgent rush. "I have to tell you that I'm crazy about you. Just... just crazy about you. I know we were supposed to just be casual. I know we weren't interested in anything serious. But I couldn't do it. I *can't* do it. I feel so much more for you than a casual fling."

She stared, swaying slightly on her feet from the shock of what she was hearing.

Vince looked utterly earnest. Just a little shy. He rambled on, "I wasn't supposed to feel this way. I've always been good at keeping things on the surface, and I thought I could with this too. I thought it was just a lust thing I'd get over quickly. I didn't want a relationship. Definitely not with you. It was all too hard and complicated. And the thing with your sister makes things awkward, but I just don't care. I have to tell you that I'm falling in love with you. I never wanted to, but I am."

Her shock was transforming as he spoke, mingling with her betrayal from before.

This was all too unbelievable.

What the hell did Vince think was going to happen right now? Just how stupid and clueless did he believe her to be?

Was he still trying to win this ridiculous game?

Her voice was sharp with irony when she finally had a chance to say something. "I'm so sorry to hear you fell for me when it's obviously the last thing you wanted."

He gave a little jerk back, like she'd hit him. "Wh-what?"

Despite herself, a pang of guilt slashed through her chest. He looked so hurt by what she'd said. Then she pushed through it because he didn't deserve her sympathy. "You've made it clear that there's nothing about me you should want, so I'm sorry that you're forced to suffer through a few feelings."

He took a physical step backward this time. They were both still in the hall in front of his open door. "This is what you're saying to me, after I—"

"After you what?" she snapped. "After you purposefully broke up Charlie and Jane, hurting both of them in the process? She had real feelings for him, and you acted

151

like she was a heartless fortune hunter! And then you ruthlessly went and took what I wanted more than anything and didn't even have the decency to tell me!"

His face was pale in emotional reaction, but at that his dark eyebrows furrowed. "What are you—"

"Don't you dare act all innocent with me! I know what you did. And you can't possibly think I'd ever return your feelings when you treat me and the people I love the way you have. From the very first day I met you, I knew you were cold and selfish and weren't even a man I could like, much less a man I could love. Yes, we had some fun together, but it was always only physical. We agreed to that from the beginning."

"I know what we agreed to." His voice was as cool now as hers was, although there was an edge of hoarseness that didn't match his hard expression. "But isn't it possible that things might change after two months?"

"If things changed, you needed to tell me that they were changing. But you didn't tell me anything. You didn't open up at all. You've lived your life making sure that nothing goes deeper than the surface, so don't you dare act aggrieved that I took you at your word."

He glanced away abruptly, taking a few ragged breaths before he spoke. "I'm sorry. I'm... sorry. This was my mistake. I thought we were getting closer."

"Well, you thought wrong. And just for future reference, if you're really getting closer to people, you don't treat them like garbage."

He flinched. She saw it before he composed his expression. "Garbage? That's really what you think of me?"

"Yes, it's what I think of you. I'm not sure how I could think anything else."

"Okay then." He stiffened his shoulders, his jaw tensely set. "If that's what you think."

"That's what I think."

"Okay then." He cleared his throat. "I won't bother you again."

He stared at her for just a moment, an ache in his eyes that almost did her in completely. Then he turned around and stepped into his condo, closing the door behind him and leaving her alone in the hall.

NINE

Two days later, Vince was staring blindly at the computer screen in the office and wondering if he was ever going to get rid of the aching knot in his stomach.

He'd had it ever since his confrontation with Liz, and it only got worse as the days, hours, minutes, and seconds passed.

He hadn't realized it was possible for his heart to hurt worse than it had when Liz was telling him exactly what she thought of him, but he'd been wrong.

His heart hurt even worse now.

He'd thought he'd done the right thing since that terrible conversation. He hadn't been pushy or needy—forcing Liz into talking to him or pressuring her to change her mind. Even though part of him wanted to plead with her to see him as he really was and not the monster she'd turned him into in her mind. And he hadn't hidden in his bedroom, moping and avoiding the world and drowning his pain in alcohol, although that was his other instinct.

He'd gone about his usual business. He'd been working hard. He'd acted normal and not let anyone know how much he was hurting.

Maybe it was to protect his pride—so Liz wouldn't know how crushed he was—but it was more to prove to himself that he could handle this.

His sister had died eight years ago. His father had died five months ago. He'd made it through both of those heartaches without falling apart.

This wasn't nearly as bad as those losses had been.

He could pull through this one without losing it.

He'd start to feel better soon. Liz wouldn't always matter to him as much as she did right now.

She couldn't.

He wouldn't be able to live the rest of his life this way.

"Vince!" The voice was loud and coming from right behind him. It surprised him so much he jumped and whirled around.

His mother. Frowning down at him. "What? What's the matter?"

"Nothing's the matter with me. I said your name four times before you heard me."

"Oh. Sorry." He blinked a few times, trying to focus. "I was out of it, I guess."

"Is that what you call it?"

"Is that what I call what?" He had no idea what was happening here, and he wasn't in an emotional state to deal with regular human interaction. He'd thought his mother was out working the register in the store, so he wasn't mentally prepared to have a lucid conversation at the moment.

She sighed and sank into the side chair next to the desk. "Vince, it might make you feel better if you talked about it."

He adjusted in his chair, trying to compose his expression. "Talk about what?"

"You know what. Why are you trying to hide it from me?"

Her gentle question was like a stab in his heart, and his heart was already too damaged to sustain it. To his embarrassment, his face twisted briefly with emotion he just couldn't control.

"Oh no, sweetie," she murmured, leaning over to touch his arm, her face reflecting deep empathy. "Is it that bad? Is there no hope at all?"

He cleared his throat and then had to clear it again. There was no point in trying to hide from his mother. She could obviously see right through him. "No. There's no hope. But I'll be fine."

"What happened? You seemed so happy, so I thought things were going well."

"The... the situation wasn't what I thought it was." There was no way in hell he was going to try to explain a no-strings-attached sexual relationship to his mother, but she'd obviously put enough pieces together to follow vague references. "It's not a big deal."

"It obviously is a big deal since you've got a broken heart."

"I don't have—" He stopped himself before he completed a lie.

There was no way to deny it.

A broken heart was exactly what he had.

"Maybe it was just too soon for her. Maybe she just needs some time. You can be patient, can't you?"

"Of course I can be patient." His voice was too rough, but he couldn't control it. "I could wait however long—but that's not the issue. She doesn't want me. She doesn't even *like* me."

"I don't believe that. I can't believe that. You wouldn't have fallen for a woman who doesn't even like you. You'd know the difference."

He thought he had, but evidently he was far stupider than he'd ever believed. "I thought we were... getting closer. But I was wrong. She said... She was so angry with me. She said I was cold and selfish. That I only thought about myself. That I could never go deep."

He didn't mean to say that much, but the words came out as the memory of Liz's lovely, bitter face slammed into him.

His mother was silent for a minute. Then her voice was very careful as she asked, "Did she know you were trying to go deep?"

"I... I told her. Everything."

"And she didn't believe you?"

He rubbed his face with his hands and tried to clear the painful blur of his mind. The conversation had been so traumatic that the details of it were obscured behind a dark cloud.

She'd been angry about Charlie and Jane, but Vince had been convinced he was helping his friend in his advice. A relationship for financial reasons—real feelings only on one side—wasn't going to make either of them happy. But Liz had implied Jane had really cared about Charlie, so maybe Vince had been wrong.

And Liz had said more than that.

"She said I took away what she wanted most," he said in a hoarse whisper, staring blankly at the old wall clock on the opposite wall.

"What did she mean?"

"I don't know." He groaned and closed his eyes. "I have no idea. She just hates me. I haven't been perfect, but I can't believe I deserve that."

His mother didn't respond.

After a couple of minutes, the silence started to feel significant, so he focused his gaze on her. Her face revealed nothing but thoughtful sympathy.

"You think she's right," he said at last. "You think I *do* deserve it."

"How would I know? I have no idea what happened. But we both know how difficult close relationships have been for you. I know you've been working on it. I know you want to do and be different. But I think it's possible that you started the relationship in your normal way, and you perhaps didn't give her enough indication that your feelings changed."

Vince stared at her, clarity hitting him hard.

Of course that was what had happened. He'd been selfish and arrogant and superficial from the beginning with Liz—exactly as she'd told him. He'd changed. Everything had changed. But maybe she didn't know that.

He hadn't opened up to her soon enough. How the hell was she supposed to know that he'd always wanted more than sex from her?

"You see what I mean, don't you?" his mother asked, patting his arm again in a comforting gesture. "That what was going on in your heart wasn't clear to her in your behavior."

He blew out a long breath and nodded. "Yes. I see what you mean. I guess I blew it."

"Maybe, but why does it have to be forever? Maybe you can talk to her again. Make things clear."

"No. It's too late. I blew it for good. She left absolutely no room for anything else." His voice broke on the last word, and it was embarrassing.

He wasn't normally like this.

He didn't like being this way.

But he was helpless against the way he was feeling right now.

"Okay. I wasn't there, so you probably know better than me. I just know that relationships are rarely that simple. And what feels final in one moment sometimes ends up being the moment that reroutes you to the future."

He started to object but stopped himself. His mother was trying to help. And the truth was the words did make him feel a little better.

"Okay. That's enough deep talk for now." Her voice was lighter now, almost breezy. "Let's talk about something else. I've got some good news."

"What's that?"

"I've made some calls over the past few days, and I've sold all the Edwards pieces in private deals. Remember those pieces you picked up the other day?"

"Really? That's great." He tried to sound encouraging, but he hardly tracked what she was saying. At the moment, business meant very little to him.

"It is. And we've made more than $50K in commission, so you should be pretty happy about that."

That got his attention. "You're kidding. That's amazing. I didn't even look at the stuff we picked up from the house. What all was it?"

"They were really amazing antiques. The kind of pieces that are really hard to find outside of high-end auctions. There was a fine Victorian bureau and an

Edwardian grand piano and the loveliest tabletop chest and—"

Vince jerked as a sliver of recognition stabbed through his exhausted brain. "*What*? What did you say?"

"What do you mean, what did I say?"

"A tabletop chest?"

"Oh, yes. It's gorgeous and incredibly rare—with birds and butterflies painted on the top."

Vince made a choking sound. "What did you say the man's name was who sold them?"

"Howard Edwards. He's in his nineties and has been holding on to those pieces for decades now, even though dealers have been pounding down his door trying to get them. I think I just caught him at the exact right time, so he sold them to me. What on earth is the matter?"

Vince felt cold, like the color had drained from his face. "Oh God. Oh *God*! No wonder she hates me so much."

"What do you mean?" His mother looked almost panicked now. "You look like you're going to pass out."

"She told me… That chest, she told me it was her favorite thing in the whole world. I had no idea it was one of the pieces. I hadn't put the names together. Oh shit, is there any way to get it back?"

"It's too late now. I'm so sorry, Vince. The deal is finalized. But this is good news, isn't it? It's all just a misunderstanding. Just explain you didn't know. If it was just a misunderstanding, then maybe you can—"

"She doesn't want to talk to me. And there was a lot more to it than a misunderstanding."

"Maybe so. But you can at least explain about the chest. I'm so sorry if something I did messed things up for you. But surely she'll forgive you if you explain you didn't know about it."

"I doubt she'd even talk to me."

"Then you have to make her hear you. Why don't you write her a letter?"

"A letter?"

"Yes. A letter. That way, it won't matter if she doesn't want to sit still and have a conversation with you. You can explain anyway, and she'll have to hear what you tell her."

Vince couldn't believe he was considering writing a letter to a woman he loved, but he had to do something. He had to make sure Liz didn't think he was such a heartless asshole as to go behind her back to acquire the piece she loved the most.

To take it away from her.

It might not change anything else, but he couldn't live with her thinking that about him.

So he gave a mute nod and dug in a drawer for a piece of paper.

His mother quietly left the office.

~

That evening, Liz found a letter on the floor of her entryway. It had obviously been slipped under the front door.

She frowned as she leaned down to pick it up, her expression deepening when she saw the word "Liz" scrawled on the otherwise blank, sealed envelope.

She'd never seen Vince's handwriting, but she knew without doubt it was from him.

She'd been going through the past few days in an exhausted daze, crying herself to sleep at night but trying to act normal during daylight hours.

One thing was clear to her now.

She'd evidently fallen in love with an asshole.

It was horrible. Humiliating. Didn't make any sense.

But even smart people were occasionally stupid.

She'd eventually get over it.

She hadn't seen Vince since their encounter in the hall on Saturday morning, and she'd been hoping to avoid him for as long as possible. It wouldn't be forever. She just wanted to recover emotionally before she confronted him again so she could present a cool, controlled demeanor and prove that he didn't mean as much to her as he thought.

God, what a fool she was.

He'd said he was falling in love with her.

Surely he couldn't have meant it. Not after he'd done what he'd done.

Even a man couldn't be so clueless as to think she'd forgive and forget the way he'd treated her, Charlie, and Jane, just because he'd abruptly declared his love.

She stared down at the closed envelope for a long time, standing in front of the front door.

She didn't want to hear what he said. She didn't want to hear anything from him ever again.

But things didn't feel settled. They didn't really make sense. There were a lot of loose ends that were driving her crazy, making her think she didn't have the full story and giving her loopholes of hope.

She couldn't keep going on that way. If this letter provided any clarity, then she needed to read it.

She needed to know.

She went to sit down on the sofa and ripped open the envelope.

She was breathing raggedly as she unfolded the piece of paper and read.

> *Liz,*
>
> *I'm not writing to ask you to change your mind. I know what we had is over for good. But I wanted to explain two things so you have the whole story. Even if we can never be together again, I can't stand for you to think so badly of me. First Charlie and Jane. I realize you think I was interfering when it wasn't my business, but Charlie is my friend, and I want him to be happy. I overheard part of a conversation that sounded like Jane was mostly interested in his money. Then I watched carefully, and as far as I could tell, Charlie was the only one with real feelings. He'd already been through a painful relationship, and I didn't want him to get hurt that way again. I thought Jane wouldn't be happy with a man she didn't love even if he happened to have money. If I was wrong in this, I am sorry. It sounded like, from what you said, that she did have real feelings. I didn't know that, and I just wanted the best for my friend. I hope you can understand that even if you don't agree with what I did.*
>
> *The other thing is the tabletop chest from Howard Edwards. Please believe that I had absolutely no idea my mother was acquiring it and the other antiques. She told me she'd gotten some pieces from a Mr. Edwards but didn't tell me what they were, and I was distracted with other things and didn't pay attention when I brought the paperwork over for him to sign. I didn't connect the name with what you'd told me. I never would have gone ahead with the deal had I realized what it included. I'm so sorry about the whole thing. My mother has*

already finalized the deal to sell the chest to a private collector, so I can't even give you the chance to buy the chest from us. I realize how much this must hurt you, but I hope you'll believe I never would have done it knowingly. I didn't understand why you were so angry when we talked, but I understand now.

I'm sorrier than you can know.

That's all I wanted to say. I won't bother you again. But I hope you won't hate me quite so much as you did before, now that you know the whole story.

Vince

Liz was sobbing when she got to the end of the letter.

The missing pieces of the story were now in place, and everything made much more sense.

Vince hadn't been trying to hurt her. He hadn't been selfish and heartless. He'd bumbled around a bit, but so had she. He'd evidently developed some real feelings for her.

And she'd still lost him for good.

It was almost worst now. It was easier when she could be genuinely angry with him. Now she was left with an overflowing mess of feelings that had absolutely no channel but tears.

She'd yelled at him for nothing.

She'd been wrong.

She'd been stupid.

She could have had him—had she listened, had she not immediately blown her top, had she not been so set on not letting him win even a single round—since his declaration of feelings was evidently sincere.

But the letter had offered no hope for a reconciliation.

She'd lost her chance with him.

She hadn't stopped crying a half hour later when Jane came in through the front door, running over as soon as she saw her sister. "Liz, what on earth is the matter?"

Liz sniffed and gasped and couldn't get any words out. She finally offered Jane the letter.

Jane read it and then slowly lifted her head. "You never told me anything was going on between you and Vince."

"I know. It wasn't supposed to mean anything."

"But it does?"

"It does. I think I... I think I..." Liz almost choked as the realization hit her.

"You love him?"

Liz nodded. "I don't know how it happened. It's too late now. It sounds like it's too late. But you see what he says about Charlie. So maybe there's a way to at least salvage that if you talk to Charlie."

Jane let out a long breath. "I don't know."

"Yes, you do. You've got real feelings for him. He might be the one. You need to tell him that. Vince's letter makes it clear that Charlie had real feelings for you too. Promise me you'll talk to him. Promise me." Liz mopped at her face. Even if she couldn't be happy in love, she'd make sure her sister would.

Jane held her eyes for a long moment before saying, "I'll do it. I'll talk to Charlie if you'll talk to Vince."

"But—"

"But what? There's nothing in this letter that says his feelings have changed. Both of you messed up. Why on earth can't it be fixed? So I'll talk to Charlie if you'll talk to Vince. That's the only way I'll do it."

Liz made a face at her sister, but her heart had sped up to a gallop. "Okay. Fine."

"Good. But both of those conversations will have to wait until tomorrow. Mom and Dad need us at home."

"What do you mean? What's going on?"

"I don't know. But Riot has been crying for two days now, and she won't come out of her room. Mom called and says she needs us to come over to help figure out what's wrong with her."

"Oh my God!" Liz groaned. "The last thing we need to be doing right now is messing around with Riot and her hysterics."

"I know. But what other choice do we have? Mom sounds desperate. Riot must have made a mess of something, and we'll have to try to fix it. What else is new?"

~

Vince didn't sleep at all that night.

He kept imagining scenarios of how Liz might have read his letter. What she might have thought. What she might do now.

He tried not to hope for impossibilities, but it was hard not to feel a flicker of it. Maybe once Liz knew the truth, she wouldn't hate him so much. Maybe she'd want to give him another chance, no matter how much he'd messed up.

Surely it wasn't completely out of the bounds of possibility.

He'd been so sure they'd had the beginnings of something good. Special.

Could he have been so pathetically wrong about the whole thing?

So he tossed and turned all night, his ears tuned for a knock on the door, any sign that Liz might be coming over to talk to him.

She didn't.

He got up early the following morning and got dressed to go to work since he couldn't sit around doing nothing and waiting any longer. When he headed down to the parking lot at six thirty in the morning, he realized his hopes for Liz to come over to talk to him last night had been futile.

Her car wasn't even here. She hadn't spent the night at home.

Maybe she was with another guy.

It wasn't likely, but even the faint possibility nauseated him.

She was free. She was allowed. But he couldn't stand the thought of her with anyone but him.

His eyes ached, and his stomach ached, and his head ached, and overall he was in a very bad mood when he got into the store.

His mother was always there early so she could sort through new inventory and redo displays. She greeted him cheerfully but didn't push when he answered with only a grunt.

He tried to distract himself with the monthly budget for an hour, but it didn't really work.

He was staring blindly at his computer in what was becoming a habit for him when his mother opened the office door. "Vince?"

"Yeah."

"There's someone here to talk to us." His mother looked and sounded worried, and he didn't understand why.

He leaned back to look beyond her and jumped to his feet when he saw Liz.

Liz.

She looked pretty and pale and red-eyed, her hair pulled into a messy ponytail.

His heart leaped in his chest. She was here. Maybe she didn't want things to be over either.

Maybe there was hope after all.

"Oh. Okay." He stood like an idiot.

Liz's face twisted. "I... I need to talk to both of you."

Vince blinked. That didn't sound right. It couldn't be what he was hoping. What did she need to talk to his mother about?

"Of course," his mom said, gesturing Liz into the office. She still looked worried, as if she'd sensed that something bad was about to happen.

She had better intuition than Vince did. He was nothing but a blank. He sat down with a thud in the desk chair while Liz and his mother took the side chairs.

Liz's posture was very straight, and she took a minute to visibly compose herself. She was really upset. So upset she could barely hold it together.

If anything was true about Liz, it was that she was always in control.

Something horrible must have happened.

Vince's stomach churned.

"I have to tell you about... about something pretty bad," Liz began, her green eyes moving from his mom to him and then back to his mom. "About Riot."

"Riot?" Vince repeated, trying to make sense of what made no sense at all.

Liz nodded. She started to talk, but a single tear slipped down her cheek. She swiped it away and stared down at her lap, almost shaking in her attempt to keep control.

It was all Vince could do not to go over and put his arms around her. She looked almost fragile, and Liz was never that.

"Dear, whatever it is, you can tell us," his mother murmured.

Liz sniffed and started again. "Riot has been… stupid. More than stupid. She's done something unforgiveable. A couple of months ago, she decided she wanted to be an expert in antiques. You know some of this. But she started buying up a bunch of stuff at auctions and sales. Pieces she thought were valuable. She's been paying way too much for them—none of them are worth much of anything—and so she's losing a ton of money. She's been doing this for a few months."

Vince waited, holding his breath. This sounded about par for the course for Riot's stupidity, but there was more. There was worse. He could see it in Liz's strained face very clearly.

"She opened a new line of credit on Berkley's account, and she's racked up a bunch of debt. A lot more than we can easily afford." Liz's voice broke, and her features contorted again before she could even them out. "But it's worse than that. She's evidently… evidently been using your company card too. Spending on it."

His mother gasped audibly, and Vince blinked.

"It's a lot," Liz rasped, staring down at her hands twisting in her lap. "I don't know how much she spent on your card. She wouldn't say. But I know it has to be a lot from the way she's acting. We're… we're going to pay you back. I promise. Before we do anything else. Just tell us how

169

much it is, and we'll do everything we can. But I'm afraid…" She wiped away a few more tears. "I'm afraid it might be more than we can cover immediately. We don't have a lot of ready cash right now. But we're putting the Pemberley House condo on the market as soon as we can. Right away. As soon as it sells, we'll hopefully have some money to deal with this mess."

She was almost sobbing now, and she had to stop talking to get control of herself.

Vince could hardly breathe. Hardly think.

Liz looked broken. It hurt him like a wound.

"Oh my dear," his mother murmured hoarsely, reaching out to pat Liz's arm the way she always did Vince's.

"It's terrible!" Liz choked. "I know it's terrible. I'm so, so sorry. All of us are. I'll understand if you want to press charges against Riot. She deserves it, and you have every right. But I did want to ask if there's any way you can let us handle this… privately. I promise we'll pay you back before we spend money on anything but our basic necessities. And I've talked to my dad and convinced him to agree to the merger deal you wanted—where you keep your name and we give ours up. If that's what it takes to fix things with you, we'll be happy to agree to that now. I'm so sorry about everything."

Liz was sobbing again, and his mother was crying too—whether out of empathy for Liz or because of the mess that was coming, Vince didn't know.

Vince knew he needed to say something, but he couldn't make his voice work.

"It's all gone." Liz was wiping away tears as she spoke. "All the love and work and time and investment we poured into Berkley's. My grandparents and my parents and me and Jane. It's all gone because of Riot. We've lost

Pemberley House. We might even have to sell my parents' house if we can't make enough from the condo. We've lost everything." She darted a quick look over at Vince for the first time since she started talking. "I've lost. Everything. Even the hope…" She trailed off whatever she was going to say. "I don't see any way to fix it. All I can do is ask that you'll give us a little time, and we'll do everything we can to make it better. And if you want to press charges against Riot, no one will blame you. Least of all me."

She stood up, shaking visibly. "I'll let you all talk about it, look over the accounts to see how much she stole from you, and figure out what you want to do from here. Riot won't come out of her room. As soon as she will, I'll make sure she apologizes in person. You can call me when you figure out where you want to go from here, and I'll make sure it happens."

Then she left the office before Vince could make himself say anything. Or even move.

"Oh my God," his mother whispered. "That poor thing."

She meant Liz.

Even though Riot had stolen from her and taken advantage of her trust, his mother's first instinct was to sympathize with Liz.

One of the reasons Vince loved her.

"Don't let her leave like that," his mother added urgently. "Go tell her it's not her fault and we'll work something out. Tell her you still love her. At least give her a hug. The poor thing is devastated. She thinks she's lost everything."

Vince blinked. Then he was suddenly, finally able to make his body work. He lurched his feet and ran through the store and outside to the sidewalk along Main Street.

But he was too late.

Liz was already pulling her car out onto the street and driving away.

TEN

Liz's whole body felt battered. Even her eyelids and her fingertips.

She'd finally stopped crying, but she was incapable of doing anything constructive. She didn't yet have the energy to go back to her parents to make plans or deal with Riot, and Jane evidently felt the same way. So for the past three hours they'd been sprawled out in their living room, occasionally talking to each other or to Em, who'd declared she wasn't going anywhere until things were fixed.

Even Anne had called from Cincinnati or Saint Louis or wherever she was currently working, but she hadn't been able to come up with a solution to this monumental disaster any more than the rest of them had.

It was terrible.

The Berkleys were ruined.

And Riot had done a lot more than devastate them financially. She might have lost them their family legacy, if they ended up having to make a deal with the Darcys. And Riot had also lost Liz the last hopes she'd had of ever fixing things with Vince.

The whole thing was so painful Liz's mind had gone numb, but she was aware enough to know that Vince hadn't called.

He'd had hours and hours now to figure things out with his mother. It couldn't be good that it was taking them so long to decide how to respond.

How would they ever be able to afford a good lawyer for Riot if the Darcys decided to press charges?

"If y'all have to sell this place," Em said from over the cup of ginger tea she'd been sipping, "then I'm going to ask Dad if we can buy it. Then we'll let you keep living here rent-free."

"Oh, Em, no," Jane murmured hoarsely. Her eyes were red from crying, but she looked a lot more pulled together than Liz herself did.

"We couldn't let you do that," Liz added.

"Why not? I don't want you to move in with your folks. You'd be so far away. What would happen to our champagne Thursdays on the terrace?"

"We'd still do them," Liz promised. "We'd just do them at your place instead."

"Dad wouldn't like that. You're not going to talk me out of this. I think it's a good—"

She broke off when a knock on the door sounded through the quiet room.

Jane straightened up, and Liz jumped to her feet, running over to get the door.

Maybe it was Vince. Maybe he'd come to talk to her in person instead of calling. She'd love for him to have chosen to do that.

When she swung open the door, it wasn't Vince's handsome, sober face that greeted her.

It was his mother's.

"Mrs. Darcy!" Her voice squeaked in surprise. "You didn't have to come all the way over. I'd have been happy to come to you."

"It's no problem. I thought a face-to-face conversation would be better than a phone call."

"Please. Come in." Liz stepped out of the way to let the older woman into the large, airy condo.

Mrs. Darcy blinked in surprise when saw Jane and Em sitting on chairs in the living room. "Oh. My goodness. I thought you'd be alone."

"Oh. We can talk in private if you'd rather."

"That might be better, given some of the things we have to talk about."

Liz stood still, trying to make her mind work, trying to follow what was happening here. She couldn't imagine why Mrs. Darcy would be saying anything that she alone needed to hear, but she wasn't about to argue since they were effectively at the woman's mercy. "That's no problem at all. We can go to my bedroom, if that's all right."

Mrs. Darcy nodded, and Liz glanced over to check with Jane's expression since her sister was as involved in this mess as she was. Jane nodded that it was fine for Liz to have the conversation in private, so Liz led Mrs. Darcy into her bedroom and gestured her into one of the two velvet rose slipper chairs in the corner.

Fortunately, the room was mostly picked up, with just a pair of shoes in the middle of the floor and the wedding dress hanging against the wall.

Mrs. Darcy wasted no time. "I'm sorry it's taken us so long to come talk to you," she began, "but Vince and I needed to work a few things out."

"Of course you did. I completely understand. You could take all the time you needed."

"I'll tell you right now, since I'm sure you and your family are sick with worry, that we don't want to press charges or go to the authorities or anything like that."

Liz had felt relatively composed, but a rush of relief hit her so hard she choked on a little sob. She covered her mouth with her hand. "Thank you! Oh thank you."

"Of course, dear. I don't see any good would come of that, except making you and Jane and your parents suffer more than you already have. And it wasn't your fault at all."

"We should have done more to restrain Riot. I knew she was too spoiled and silly and out of control, but there wasn't anything—" She broke off the words since she didn't want it to sound like she was making excuses.

"She's your sister. Of course you couldn't control her. She's responsible for her own decisions. Vince and I have gone over the credit card statements for the past three months. I wish we'd caught it earlier, but I'm afraid I never pay attention to the financial stuff, and Vince is just getting used to the business and wouldn't have been able to recognize which purchases weren't legitimate."

"Of course not. It's all Riot's fault. So you figured out how much she owes you?"

Mrs. Darcy nodded and handed Liz a printout.

Liz took the page with slightly shaking hands and stared down at it for a few seconds before she could get her vision to focus.

When she'd processed the number, she closed her eyes and blew out a slow breath.

"Is it what you were expecting?" Mrs. Darcy asked.

Liz opened her eyes. "Honestly, it's not as bad as I was imagining. This is... this is a relief."

"I'm so glad. It wasn't as much as Vince and I were expecting either."

"It's more than we currently have available in the bank, but if you'll give us a few weeks, we're going to sell some of our personal antiques, and then we should easily have enough to pay you back this amount in cash."

Mrs. Darcy had very kind eyes. Much kinder than Liz felt like they deserved. "And we're happy to take it, if that's what you and your parents think best, but Vince and I worked out another option, if you'd like to hear it."

"Another option?"

"I raised three children myself, and I understand how families work. How sometimes we cover for others because we love them. How we'll pay the price that they owe. Riot is the one who owes us—not the rest of you—so we'd rather the rest of you not be forced to pay off her debt. So we can arrange it so she continues to work for us—at the same hourly rate she's earning now—until she pays off the debt."

"Oh, but you can't possibly want her to still work for you! You'd never be able to trust her."

"Not at the cash register, no. She'd have to work in our storeroom. We have all kinds of inventory there that needs to be organized and cataloged. Piles of small items that people dump on us but aren't valuable enough to sort through right away. I'm sure you have a similar situation yourself. No one's ever wanted to take the time to sort it all out, so it's one of those things that never gets done. But she could do that. Fred is in charge of our inventory and storeroom, so he'd supervise her. He's quite the taskmaster, so he wouldn't let her get into any trouble."

Liz twisted her hands in her lap, trying to steady her voice and features. "I'll talk to my parents, but I'm sure they'd agree that this is a very generous offer. I don't want take advantage of your kindness though, after the way Riot—"

"Oh, dear, you're not taking advantage of us at all. I actually wanted to write off the whole thing, but Vince said that wouldn't be good for Riot, to not face any consequences, and of course he's right. I'm sure she won't enjoy working in the storeroom, but maybe it will be a learning experience."

"I sure hope so. I hope, when she realizes that her other option is to be arrested, she'll work her hardest to pay off the debt."

Mrs. Darcy chuckled softly. "We can hope. Either way, I think it's the best option for all concerned. I'm so glad Vince thought of it."

Liz lowered her eyes and pushed back a few waves of hair that had escaped her messy ponytail. "So Vince didn't want to come talk this out too?"

"He thought it would be best, given the situation, if I came alone. He didn't want you to feel any extra pressure."

That didn't sound too bad. That didn't sound like he hated her.

"We also have another thing to show you. Regarding the idea of a merger."

Liz stiffened. "Oh. Of course. If you want to go through with that merger, naturally we'll do it. If the deal with Riot is contingent on—"

"Of course it's not contingent! What must you think of us? Anyway, this isn't the agreement we were pushing for in the past. This is different. Berkley's would be able to keep its name." Mrs. Darcy handed Liz a thin stack of papers. "Vince worked this out. It's why it took us a few hours to come talk to you."

Liz scanned the top sheet blindly, having trouble focusing on the letters on the page and understanding the words she was reading.

When it finally processed, she made a choking sound in her throat. "This is too much. Too generous."

"No, it's really not. Vince assured me it was fair. Berkley's has a history and a reputation in this area that Darcy's will never have. This is perfectly fair, if you and your parents would like to sell out. The Berkley name would remain."

Liz didn't want to, no matter how generous the offer. She loved the store, and she loved what she did, and giving it up—even in a crisis like this—would feel to her like a failure. But it wasn't just her decision to make. "I'll have to talk to Jane and my dad and…" She trailed off. She was afraid if she showed this to her mother, the size of the figure they'd receive would be too tempting for her mother to refuse. Then they'd lose control of the business, and her mother would start spending like crazy.

The money would be gone before they knew it.

Maybe she'd just talk to Jane and her dad to begin with.

"Of course. Take your time. Just know that it's a possibility. I know you said Riot accumulated debt on your own credit line, and you're having to deal with that too.

"Yes. But if you're okay with Riot working for you, then we might be able to raise enough cash for the rest of the debt by selling Riot's car and some of our best antiques." She glanced behind her at the beloved wedding dress hanging on the wall. "I'm selling that dress."

"Oh no, dear!"

"I need to. It's an indulgence I just can't justify. It's not like I'm getting married and will need that dress anytime soon. I think it will bring a lot of money."

"Of course it will. If you're going to sell it, then sell it to me."

"I couldn't—"

"Why not? This is what I do. Find the best acquisitions." She got up and walked over to inspect the dress. "This is amazing craftsmanship. You have to let me have it. Don't sell it to anyone else."

"Of course you can have it if you want it. I paid—"

"I'm not going to take it from you at cost. That's ridiculous. You could sell it to someone else and actually make money on it." She reached into her purse and pulled out a checkbook. Then she quickly wrote out a check, tore it out, and handed it to Liz. "What about this? Is that fair?"

Liz made a squeak. "It's too much! It's twice what I paid!"

"And I'll be able to turn around and get twice that amount when I sell this to a customer. I'm not being nice here. This is a business deal, and you'll hurt my feelings if you don't accept my offer."

Liz's stomach twisted, but she didn't know how she could say no. She didn't even want to say no. "Okay. I'll take it. Thank you so much." She quickly took the dress and zipped it up in the garment bag it had come in, giving the silky fabric a few fond strokes before she did so.

She loved that dress so much.

But her family was more important.

Even Riot. The stupid, stupid girl.

"Excellent. Now that's settled, I'll be off." Mrs. Darcy folded the garment bag over her arm when Liz handed it to her. "Just let us know what your family thinks about the offer."

"I will. And I'll have Riot come over and work out a schedule for getting started on her new job." Liz paused. Took a ragged breath before she added, "Please thank Vince for me."

"I will."

"And… and thank him for the letter he sent me. I understand if he doesn't want to talk to me now, but could you please tell him that I'm sorry I misunderstood."

Mrs. Darcy's face softened. "I'll tell him."

Her expression was too sympathetic. Like she knew Liz's feelings for Vince and felt sorry for her.

Vince and his mother were good people, and so they were being generous in a difficult situation. But that didn't mean Vince still loved her.

There was a moment when she might have had everything she'd ever wanted. When Vince might have been within reach. But she'd blown it.

She'd lost her chance with him.

~

Vince was trying to work while his mother went to talk to Liz, but he was too anxious and jittery to concentrate on anything. He paced around. Played on his phone. Visualized how the conversation might be going.

Hoped that Liz was all right.

It was harder than he'd expected not to talk to her himself, but the last thing he wanted to do was complicate matters with the messiness between him and Liz. And he definitely didn't want her to think that their offer to her family was based on an expectation that she be in a relationship with him.

He just wanted to help her—whether he was ever allowed to be with her again or not.

When he heard the bell jangle on the front door of the store, he jumped out of his chair and left the office, relieved that the newcomer was indeed his mother.

She was carrying a garment bag, which was strange.

"What did she say?" Vince demanded.

"Let me at least get in and sit down before you interrogate me." His mom was smiling. That had to be a good sign.

He bit back his questions and waited until his mother was settled in a chair in the office. Then he asked again, "What did she say?"

"She was very happy about the idea of Riot working off the debt. She was sure her parents would agree, so I think that's settled. She wasn't sure about the rest of the offer. She said she'd talk to her family about it and let us know. I don't think she wants to, but she'll do it if it's the best choice for her family."

"You told her they could keep the Berkley name?"

"Of course. But she loves the work."

"Yeah, but she could still work for—"

"Vince, it's not your decision. It's theirs."

"I know. Thanks for going along with it."

His mother laughed. "You know I never handle the money stuff. As long as I keep my store, I couldn't care less what you do with the business stuff."

"So how did Liz look? Okay?"

She reached out and patted his arm. "She was upset, but she looked better. She was really relieved about not having to come up with the cash to pay us. She and her family are selling Riot's car and a bunch of their antiques, and she said they might be able to come up with enough to cover the rest of Riot's debt. So it sounds like they might not have to sell Pemberley House."

"Oh shit, that would be great. Liz loves that place."

"I know. And it would be terrible for her and Jane to have to lose what they love in order to protect their sister. Hopefully it will work out."

Vince was feeling better but just as restless as before. Like it took effort to even sit still. "What's in that bag?"

"This is a wedding dress that Liz sold to me."

"What?" Vince lurched to his feet and unzipped the garment bag enough to see the dress. "Mom! You bought her dress? She loves this dress! She's crazy about it! How could you let her sell—"

"Vince." His mother's voice was soft, but it stopped him nonetheless.

"What?"

"Give me a little credit."

"For what?"

"For not being an idiot and for not snatching a dress out of from under a desperate young woman who loves it. If I didn't buy the dress, she'd have sold it to someone else. And then we wouldn't have it when we need it."

Vince blinked. "When we..."

"Need it. To give back to her."

Vince held on to the back of a chair so he wouldn't sway on his feet. "Mom."

"Don't Mom me. I know what I'm doing. I told you all along that you need a wife. Now we have the dress ready for when the time comes."

"But I don't... But I'm not... She's not... We're not..."

"See, that's where you're wrong." She spoke as if what he'd just babbled out had been a complete, coherent thought. "I don't think things are as hopeless as you believe them to be. She was very disappointed that you didn't want to talk to her yourself."

"She was?" He could hear the raw note of desperation in his voice, but he couldn't control it.

"Yes. She was. I think she was hoping to talk to you. And maybe talk about more than just Riot. So I've got the wedding dress for when you need it."

"Mom, you didn't hear what she said to me."

"That was before. She thanked you for the letter. She said she's sorry she misunderstood. Things are different now."

His vision was blurring. His heart was racing. He wanted more than anything to believe what his mother was saying was the truth.

But he wasn't sure he could believe it.

"Vince, listen to me. I'm your mom. I love you. I'm not going to convince you of something that's not true. I know you were hurt. I know you tried for the first time to go deep, and you ended up with a broken heart. But that's what happens when you feel things for real. Sometimes you get hurt. But the thing is, you don't *always* get hurt. And you can never have everything unless you're prepared to risk losing everything. So I'm telling you this now. Try one more time with Liz."

Vince swallowed over an ache in his throat. His hand clenched around the top of the chair back. He couldn't move.

"Vince, it's worth it. I promise it is. Try one more time."

He gave a jerky nod. Took a loud, hoarse breath.

Then he summoned what was left of his courage and returned to Pemberley House to find Liz.

~

Liz and Jane called their father to talk about the Darcys' offer, and the three of them decided they'd accept it if they had no other choice, but first they wanted to see how much money they could raise in the next few weeks to cover the debt.

Her father wasn't ready to give up Berkley's, and Liz and Jane didn't want to either.

If they could make things work otherwise, then they'd keep it.

Once that was concluded, Liz felt more settled. She was still exhausted and sad and drained and wistful, but she was no longer on the verge of falling apart. So she took a book to her favorite spot in the far corner of the estate, and she lay on one of the lounges and pretended to read.

Mostly she closed her eyes and thought about Vince.

"Liz." The familiar voice seemed to come out of her imagination since she'd just been picturing his face.

She froze and listened. It had sounded so real.

"Liz? Are you asleep?"

She popped up into a sitting position, her eyes flying open. "Vince?"

He was standing a few feet away from her, dressed in khakis and a French-blue Oxford. His expression was very sober. "Yes. It's me."

"What— I didn't expect you." She tried to smooth down her hair, but it was hopeless. Frizzy waves were everywhere. She probably looked terrible.

"I know. I went to your place, and Jane said you were out here."

"I am."

"I know. I found you."

They stared at each other.

It was a minute before Liz could pull herself together. "Thank you," she managed to say. "For everything. For Riot and for—"

"You don't have to thank me."

"Yes, I do. Your mom said it was all your idea."

"She shouldn't have said that." He stepped over, hesitated a few seconds, and then lowered himself to sit on the side of the lounge beside her. "It was my mom too. She's amazing. We wanted to work things out in a way that was fair but that didn't make you and the rest of your family suffer for something that wasn't your fault."

"You did work it out. And I can't thank you enough."

"I don't want you to thank me." His gray eyes were deeper than she remembered. Filled with something she could barely recognize.

"Well, I'm going to do it anyway. You have no idea what a difference it makes for us. How much it takes the burden off us."

Vince inclined his head. Then darted a quick look up at her through his dark lashes. "I'm glad it helped you. I did it for you."

She gasped, hardly daring to believe she'd heard him correctly. She shifted her position and grew tense.

Vince cleared his throat. "I wasn't sure I should... I don't know if you want to hear anything from me again. About my... my feelings. But I'm going to say this one more time. And if you say no again this time, then I'll never bother you with this again. But I love you, Liz. I love you. I know I messed it up before. I know I kept things to myself and didn't let you know my feelings were changing. And then I blurted them out to you out of nowhere when you had no reason to expect it. But I think I can do better. I want to do better."

She hugged her arms to her belly, trying to hold back the swell of intense feeling. "You… you do?"

"Yes, I do. I don't want to give up on you, just because I messed up before. I want everything. I want you— as much as I can get, as deep as I can get. And I'll give you everything that's in me too. If you… if you want it."

She gave a little sob and had to cover her face with her hands. But when she lowered them, she was smiling through tears. "I do! Vince, I do."

He gave a little jerk. "You do?"

"Yes!" She flung herself toward him so he had to wrap his arms around her. She clung to his shirt. "I love you too. I didn't know it. I kept trying to be just as cool and casual as you were about our relationship so you wouldn't win or something stupid like that. But it was all a futile effort. I fell in love with you too. I want everything with you. I know it now for sure."

He made a choked sound in his throat. The most helpless sound she'd ever heard from him. His arms tightened almost brutally around her for a few seconds until he loosened his hug but didn't pull away.

She buried her face in his shirt. "I'm so sorry I thought the worst of you. I should have known you'd never take that chest away from me on purpose."

"I wouldn't. I promise I wouldn't. But I'm so sorry you lost it because of us."

"That's okay. You didn't know. I loved that chest. And I loved that wedding dress. But I love you more than them."

He lifted his head to peer down at her. "You do?"

She giggled and cupped his face with one hand. "Yes. I do."

"So you'll be my girlfriend now? For real? I can let everyone know?"

"Yes. For real. And you better believe everyone will know, because as soon as I tell Em, it'll be all over. The whole town will know within an hour."

He chuckled. "That's okay with me." He hugged her again, and this time they ended up reclining together on the lounge. Liz had no complaints about the position. "I am sorry about Jane and Charlie," Vince added.

"I know. I told Jane she needed to talk to Charlie. I really think they can work things out since it was just a misunderstanding."

"I talked to Charlie earlier. I told him it was my mistake and he shouldn't give up on Jane. I think he was planning to call her today."

"Oh good. I'm so happy to hear that. They're really good together."

"Yes. They are. Almost as good together as we are."

"Oh no. I think they're better than we are."

"What?" Vince was stroking her back and hair with an almost sappy smile on his face. "How could they be better together than we are?"

"Well, for one, they don't get into ridiculous fights about nothing. And two, they don't spend all their time trying to one-up each other. And three…"

"I don't need to hear a three. I think what you're saying is that they win as a couple." His voice was warm and amused. Teasing.

Liz frowned. "No. I didn't say they win."

"So *we* win?"

"Yes, we win. Because we told each other 'I love you' first."

He burst into laughter and pressed a few light kisses against her lips. "All right. It's settled. We win."

~

A month later, Vince was in a warm state of physical and emotional pleasure as he kissed Liz in the back seat of his SUV at seven thirty on a Friday morning.

He was trying not to get too aroused, given their location and situation, so he made sure to keep his hands on her face and hair, restraining the urge to let them slide lower. Liz apparently hadn't set any such boundaries on the roaming of her little hands. One of them was making a slow route down his back and lower to his butt, squeezing him there over his trousers.

"Liz," he managed to say over her lips.

"What?" She sounded faintly annoyed as she claimed his mouth again.

He pulled farther back. "I'm getting turned on. Are you really sure you want to pursue that particular course of action right now?" He was pleased to hear a familiar dry irony in his tone.

She giggled and pulled away, dropping her hands as she leaned back against the seat. "Fine. Always so horny. Won't let me have any fun."

"Horny?" His arched his eyebrows.

"Eager," she amended.

He lifted his eyebrows even higher.

"Okay. Passionate. Happy now?"

"Very."

He was, despite the lingering pulsing of arousal in his blood, he was amused and content and affectionate. Four months ago, he'd never have believed he was capable of feeling this way—as if all the unfulfilled emotion he'd kept in a tight safe ball had finally found a reason for existing.

It was Liz. Much of it was Liz.

But not all of it. Everything in his life felt bigger and realer and happier now that he could let himself feel, invest, live.

Go deep.

His mother had been right all along.

He gave Liz a lopsided grin that made her laugh again. She reached over to take his hand.

"We've still got a half hour before the door opens. Now that you've ruined our fun, what are we supposed to do to amuse ourselves?" She pulled her phone out of her purse and glanced down at it idly.

Evidently she'd gotten a text because she tapped out a quick reply.

"Who is it?" he asked.

"Jane. She and Charlie had an argument this morning."

"Oh yeah? I can just imagine what it looked like. He probably frowned at her, and then she burst into tears, and then he spent about an hour apologizing."

Liz snickered. "Pretty much. They have no idea what arguing really looks like. We're way better at it than them."

"No doubt about that." Vince had never seen his friend as happy as he was with Jane, and he didn't want anything to get in the way of that, so he added, "Did Jane and Charlie work things out?"

"Yes. It sounds like it was just a little thing. They made up before Charlie left for school."

"Good." He rearranged so he could stretch out his legs, his eyes making a casual path around the cars parked along the driveway of the big house. "Did I tell you my mom said Riot didn't leave work until after ten last night?"

"No! She stayed that late?"

"Yes. She was almost finished with her inventory of those old dishes. You know that mountain that kept collecting that we could never get organized? She wanted to finish it before she left."

Liz chuckled, her face reflecting a fond amusement that did Vince's heart good to see. "She really has devoted herself to her duties. Em has decided that what Riot needs is a mentor, and ever since she's taken on the job, Riot does seem to be better focused. As crazy as it sounds to have Em as a mentor, maybe what Riot needed was a good influence that wasn't one of her sisters. Part of me still thinks her penitence is just another role she's putting on, that she's enjoying the drama of it. But who the hell cares as long as it lasts until she's worked off her debt."

"Exactly. She's done a good job. Mom is thrilled since she sees it as a personal victory. And I'm just glad I'm not the one supervising her."

"I'm glad about that too. If she was around you too much, I have these visions of her deciding she's secretly in love with you and she'd start acting out a doomed, tragic passion." Liz's lip curled up in a snarl. "I wouldn't like that at all."

He laughed as he brought her hand up to his mouth to kiss her knuckles one by one. "That doesn't seem likely to happen. I don't think she likes me very much. And besides, it wouldn't matter since I'm already taken."

"Yes, you are. And everyone better realize it."

"I think they do. Girls don't come on to me nearly as much as they used to."

Liz frowned. "They still come on to you?"

"Occasionally, but not as much as they used to. I must now project a taken vibe that scares them off."

"Well, start working on ramping up your taken vibe. They shouldn't be coming on to you at all." Liz's face was set in what Vince knew was her competitive expression. "Next time one does, you tell me about it. I'll make sure she keeps her hands off."

"No one's hands are on me but yours." The surge of pleased possessiveness was familiar to Vince now. He liked it. A lot. The certain knowledge that Liz was his and he was hers. He wasn't sure how he'd lived so long without it. "No need to compete with all these random women who don't happen to know that I'm not available."

"All these women? You said it only happened occasionally! Exactly how often are you getting hit on?"

He burst into laughter and pulled her into a hug. In just a few seconds, her body relaxed. They sat together in perfect satisfaction for a few minutes until Liz straightened up and pulled out her phone.

"Okay. We'll need to get back up to the door soon."

"We've got almost twenty minutes before they open the doors."

"I know, but I want to make sure we're in position. Here. I'm pulling up the listing. Let's go over our plan of attack."

"I already know which pieces I'm responsible for getting."

"It won't hurt to go over it again." She showed him a photograph on the phone. "This is the Brandt painting in the dining room. I saw George Kent in line, and I think he'll be in the first group. He's going to be going for the painting too, so you'll have to beat him. You grab that painting, no matter what they've priced it."

Vince managed to hide a smile at Liz's serious expression. "Got it."

"When you've gotten that, you go to the dining room and grab any of the carved figurines you can that are priced under a hundred dollars. More than that, and they won't be worth it. I'll come back on Sunday and see if anything is left at a discount."

"Got it. Painting. Then figurines."

"And I'll go upstairs and claim the armoire. Then I'll check the shoes and handbags." She rubbed her hands together excitedly. "This is going to be a good one. I can feel it. I'm glad I won the coin toss."

They'd made an agreement to take turns at big estate sales like this so they wouldn't be in competition with each other. Liz's family had decided to keep ownership of Berkley's for the time being since they'd gotten their finances under control, and Vince knew Liz was happy about it. Maybe things would change in the future, but for now they were working for different stores.

"If we can get the good stuff here and can sell it on at a good price, we might have enough to pay off the rest of Riot's debt." Liz was putting her phone in her purse and organizing herself, putting on her game face. "I don't think we'll have to sell Pemberley House."

"Good. I'm glad." Vince shook his head fondly. Liz was about to enter her full-fledged competitive stance, the one where she forgot about everything else in the world. Including him.

Then she surprised him by turning to meet his eyes. "Just so you know, we'd never have been able to get to this point if it hadn't been for you."

His heart clenched. "It wasn't just me."

"It was mostly you." She leaned over to kiss him softly. "You saved us, Vince. Don't think I'll ever forget it."

He hadn't expected to be hit with this kind of emotion right at this moment, and he wasn't prepared for it. He cleared his throat and glanced away. "I didn't do that much."

"Yes, you did. You saved us."

He leaned forward to kiss her back. "If that's the case, it's only because you saved me first."

Their gazes met across the few inches of distance as they pulled back from the kiss, and Vince saw everything he needed to know about her heart, their love, their future in her eyes.

Then Liz pulled them out of the car so they could be first in line for the estate sale.

They'd arrived together, and Liz had passed out the numbers.

She was Number One, and he was Number Two.

Vince wouldn't have it any other way.

EPILOGUE

Six months later, Liz woke up when Vince started to get out of bed.

It was still early—too early—so she reached out to grab him. She was still mostly asleep, but she managed to hook her fingers around the waistband of his sleep pants.

She held on as the fabric stretched.

He fell back into bed with a grunt. "That was uncalled for."

She giggled and blinked in the dark room. "What's uncalled for is you getting up at the crack of dawn. Why are you awake so early?"

"I thought we were going to the estate sale." He was bare-chested and his hair was a mess, kinked in all directions. He shouldn't have looked sexy right now, but he did.

She made a face at him. "I'm rethinking it now. I'm not sure there will be anything good there, and I'd rather sleep in this morning."

"You're awake now, so you might as well get up." Vince sounded (rather annoyingly) alert this morning, which was unusual since she was usually an earlier riser than he was.

She yanked at his pants again and was gratified when he rolled over on top of her with a wolfish smile. "Now," she said, spreading her thighs to make room for his body. "That's better."

"You really want to have sex before six o'clock in the morning, before you've even brushed your teeth?"

This reminder of the possible state of her breath made her scowl. "Sometimes you don't mind."

"I'm not saying I mind. I'm asking if that's really what you want to do right now, or are you just trying to think of a reason to keep me in bed."

He was way too smart. Way too quick.

He always had been.

He was the only man she'd ever known who could mentally outmaneuver her.

Sometimes. Not all the time.

She'd just woken up, so she wasn't at her best at the moment.

"What's wrong with that?"

"Nothing's wrong with that." His expression softened as he pressed a little kiss against her lips. "I'll have sex with you any time, any place, in any condition. Just say the word. But if you don't want to go to the estate sale, just say so. You don't have to offer sex as an alternative."

She giggled and wrapped her arms around him in a tight hug. "I love you. You know that, right?"

"I've been informed of that fact on more than one occasion, but I'm always happy for a refresher."

"I love you," she said again, her chest tightening with emotion. She'd never known what it was like to love in this particular way. To feel that this man and all his intelligence and depth and heart and sharp edges were hers. *Hers.* Responding to the strength of the emotion, she added, "And you know you can move in with me if you want, after Charlie and Jane get married."

Jane and Charlie had gotten engaged last night. Liz was very excited for them, but the upcoming marriage would mean a change in their living situation. Jane would naturally move in with Charlie, which meant Vince would need to live somewhere else.

Vince's eyes were very serious as he said, "I didn't know until you told me just now. I didn't want to assume I could move into someone else's home."

"Well, you can. I'd love to have you move in here." She cleared her throat as she realized what she was saying. How serious it was. "If you want. There's no pressure or anything. I know we're on a different timetable than Jane and Charlie. I mean, just because they're engaged doesn't mean we have to... we have to make a big step too. You don't have to move in with me. Or you could just take Jane's room if you'd rather. If you want your own room. I mean..." She trailed off, feeling like an idiot. She was usually better at talking than this, but she was buffeted with a wave of nerves and self-consciousness.

Vince burst into laughter and wrapped his arms around her, rolling them both onto their sides. "If the invitation was a serious one and not something you accidentally stumbled into, then I'd love to move in with you."

"Oh good. It was serious. I know I started rambling on afterward, but that was because I was suddenly afraid you'd think it was too much, too soon."

"It's not too much. I want to live with you."

She found his mouth and kissed him. Not deeply, but tenderly. "I want to live with you too."

"Then that's settled." Vince let her go and rolled to the side of the bed, hefting himself up with a soft groan.

She popped up into a sitting position. "You still want to go to that dumb estate sale? We could hang out this morning and talk about our upcoming cohabitation. It might not be as exciting as Jane and Charlie getting engaged, but it's still—"

Vince turned his head toward her sharply. "You're not feeling competitive, are you?"

"About what?"

"About Jane and Charlie beating us to the altar."

"Oh. No. No! I know we're not—" She broke off because the truth was she was more than ready to marry Vince. She didn't want to lie to him and say she wasn't, but she also didn't want him to feel pressure.

If he ever asked her to marry him, she wanted it to come from nothing but a desire to do so. She wasn't going to guilt or push him into it.

She started again. "We're not Jane and Charlie. We don't have to do what they do. I'm incredibly happy exactly as we are, and I'll be even happier when you move in here with me. I'm not looking to beat Jane to anything else."

He nodded, his lip twitching up slightly as if something she'd said amused him. "Okay then. If we want to be first in line for the estate sale, we need to get moving. I'll get coffee."

"But I was serious about wondering if we should even bother."

He'd stood up, but he paused at her words. "You really don't want to go? It's your turn to get the good stuff."

"I know."

"We can skip this one if you want, but I still get the stuff at the next one."

She gasped in outrage.

His lips twitched up again. "It's only fair."

She snarled. "Okay. Fine. But I'm not moving from this bed until you bring me coffee."

Vince was chuckling as he left the room. He really was awake and in a good mood particularly early this morning.

She called out to his back, "And not the easy stuff. You have to use the french press!"

He laughed even more. But the coffee he brought back to her several minutes later was perfect.

~

They were leaving the building about a half hour later, and Liz was getting into her competitive mood, ready to beat everyone else to the best items at the sale.

She wasn't paying attention, so she almost ran smack into Em at the front entrance.

It was way too early on a Saturday morning for Em to be out and about yet. Plus she was wearing silk pajamas and a soft pink bathrobe.

What the hell was she doing coming back into the building at this time?

And why was Ward Knightley behind her.

Knightley was around forty, and he was a good-looking, easygoing man. He had a large frame, thick brown hair, and thoughtful blue eyes. This morning he was wearing plaid flannel pants and a T-shirt it looked like he'd just pulled on.

Liz gaped at them.

"What's the matter with you?" Em asked, looking innocently from Liz to Vince. "You look like someone just socked you in the gut."

"What are you doing?" Liz asked, her eyes running up and down Em's slim body again to verify that she was indeed in her pajamas and coming back into the building with Knightley.

"Oh, I was just—" Em stopped short, as if the appearance had just occurred to her. She burst into laughter. "Oh my God, you should see your face! Do you think I spent the night with Ward or something?"

She evidently found that idea hilarious because she couldn't stop laughing about it.

Knightley shook his head and rolled his eyes in an ironically amused expression. "She has a plumbing problem. She came out to get me."

Liz laughed at his quite reasonable explanation for the situation. "Oh. That makes sense. I was wondering. But why didn't you just call him?"

"I tried. Three times. He wouldn't answer."

"I was asleep."

Em went on. "So I had to go all the way out and rouse him from bed. Talk about grumpy."

"What's the plumbing problem?"

"It's just a clogged sink. I unclogged it, but Dad is in a dither about it, and he won't settle down until we get Ward out to make sure it's fixed." Em was the only person who ever called him Ward. Everyone else called him Knightley. "You know Dad."

"Yes. Hopefully you can quickly confirm that it's unclogged, and poor Knightley can go back to bed."

"Too late now," he muttered.

Liz and Em both giggled at that, and Vince cleared his throat. "We better get going if we want to be first in line."

"Okay. Fine. I don't know why you're all uptight about this sale. One would think *you* were the competitive one." Liz touched Em's arm. "I'll see you later."

"Definitely. We've got a wedding to start planning!" Em looked as excited about it as if she were the one getting married.

Liz watched her friend disappear into the building. "Do you suppose Em managed to get into Knightley's cottage to wake him up, or did she just bang on the door really loud?"

"I have no idea. He's used to catering to her father, and he didn't really look annoyed by it. Now let's get moving."

"Fine. We're moving. All I've got to say is that there better be some good stuff at this sale for all your pestering me about it."

"We'll see."

~

They were the first people in line. They hadn't really needed to hurry.

In fact, they were still the only people waiting when Farrah arrived at seven thirty, grinning at Liz as she approached.

"You're early," Liz said, checking the time. The staff from this company usually didn't arrive until an hour before the sale was set to begin.

"Yeah. Just happened that way. No one else here yet?"

"No. Just Vince and me."

"Well, since you came so early, I'll let you guys in to look around right now. Just don't tell anyone else I let you do it."

"Seriously?" Liz clapped her hands, excited as she always was about getting a leg up on the competition.

"Sure. Why not? Take ten minutes to look around, but then come back out and wait in line. You can't actually buy anything until the sale begins."

Liz didn't even question her good fortune. She just walked into the house, holding Vince's hand.

"Let's start upstairs," Vince said.

"Okay." She'd have started on the main floor, but it didn't really matter to her where they started.

Vince led her up the stairs and then walked into what was obviously the master bedroom.

"There are some really good pieces here," she said, eyeing the sleigh bed and carved armoire with a practiced eye.

"Yes."

Liz jerked to a stop as her eyes landed on the long dresser against the wall.

On top of it was a tabletop chest.

A beautiful cedar chest with watercolors of birds and butterflies on the top.

"What's the matter?" Vince asked.

"Look at that!"

"At what?"

"The chest. The chest! That looks just like the one... the one I loved that Mr. Edwards... Oh my God, it's exactly the same." She ran over to look at it. "It *is* the same. It has to be the same. But how on earth did it end up here? I thought you said your mom sold it to a private collector."

"She did."

"Then how... There couldn't possibly be another..." She couldn't even get a full sentence out. Her body was throbbing with excitement. She ran her fingers over the smooth surface.

It was beautiful.

Perfect.

Exactly what she'd always wanted.

She looked up at Vince and gasped at what she saw in his eyes.

"Vince?" Her voice broke.

"Maybe you should open it," he murmured hoarsely.

Her hands started to tremble as she reached out to open the top of the chest.

Inside, resting on the deep red velvet, was a ring. An antique. It looked Edwardian with its elaborately engraved mounting and a beautiful round diamond.

It was an engagement ring.

She stared down at it, something deep inside her shuddering.

"If it's too soon," Vince murmured beside her, "I can hold it. I can wait. For as long as you need."

She reached out for the ring greedily, like someone might snatch it away. "No! I want it now!"

Vince made a choking sound. It might have been laughter. But when she looked up at him, his eyes were deep and full. "I love you, Liz. I want to go deep. All the way. As deep as we can get. Forever. So I want you to be my wife, if you could ever want me for a husband."

She threw herself against him, the ring clenched tightly in her hand. "Yes! Yes, yes, yes! I want to be your wife more than anything!"

He hugged her so tightly she could barely breathe, but then he released her and was laughing when he pulled away. "So I can put the ring on your finger?"

"Oh. Yes. Please." She handed him the ring and then presented him her left hand.

He was grinning as he slid the ring onto her finger. It fit exactly right, so he must have asked Jane for her size or else investigated her jewelry box on his own.

"Is that really my same chest?" she asked, looking back at the beloved item, almost as precious to her as the ring she wore.

"Yes. I bought it back from the man my mother sold it to."

"Oh no! It must have been so expensive for him to give it up again."

"It wasn't too expensive. I wanted you to have it. You can call it an engagement gift."

She was so emotional as she caressed the chest that she was afraid she might tear up. Fortunately, Vince distracted her before she did.

"So now that that's settled, I can show you this." Vince opened the closet door.

There was only one thing inside. A wedding dress hanging on the bar.

A wedding dress she knew very well.

It was too much.

She burst into tears and ended up crying against Vince's chest. "I thought your mom sold it," she gurgled when she was finally able to form words.

"She didn't. She bought it so she could give it to me and so I could give it back to you. She knew we'd be getting here from the very beginning. So she wanted us to have this."

"I feel like I've gotten everything I ever wanted."

Vince leaned down to kiss her. "So have I. Because I have you."

They kissed and hugged and generally made fools of themselves for a few more minutes. But there was actually an estate sale happening in this house today. Vince had evidently arranged this little surprise, but they couldn't spend all morning up in this room.

So Liz and Vince collected her chest and her wedding dress and started downstairs.

Liz was still wearing the ring, and Vince was holding her hand.

She decided they could forego the rest of the sale.

There wasn't anything left she could possibly want.

ABOUT NOELLE ADAMS

Noelle handwrote her first romance novel in a spiral-bound notebook when she was twelve, and she hasn't stopped writing since. She has lived in eight different states and currently resides in Virginia, where she writes full time, reads any book she can get her hands on, and offers tribute to a very spoiled cocker spaniel.

She loves travel, art, history, and ice cream. After spending far too many years of her life in graduate school, she has decided to reorient her priorities and focus on writing contemporary romances. For more information, please check out her website: noelle-adams.com.

Books by Noelle Adams

Pemberley House
> In Want of a Wife
> If I Loved You Less
> Loved None But You

Trophy Husbands
> Part-Time Husband
> Practice Husband
> Packaged Husband

The Loft Series
> Living with Her One-Night Stand

Living with Her Ex-Boyfriend
Living with Her Fake Fiancé

Holiday Acres
Stranded on the Beach
Stranded in the Snow
Stranded in the Woods
Stranded for Christmas

One Fairy Tale Wedding Series
Unguarded
Untouched
Unveiled

Tea for Two Series
Falling for her Brother's Best Friend
Winning her Brother's Best Friend
Seducing her Brother's Best Friend

Balm in Gilead Series
Relinquish
Surrender
Retreat

Rothman Royals Series
A Princess Next Door
A Princess for a Bride
A Princess in Waiting
Christmas with a Prince

Preston's Mill Series (co-written with Samantha Chase)

Roommating
Speed Dating
Procreating

Eden Manor Series
One Week with her Rival
One Week with her (Ex) Stepbrother
One Week with her Husband
Christmas at Eden Manor

Beaufort Brides Series
Hired Bride
Substitute Bride
Accidental Bride

Heirs of Damon Series
Seducing the Enemy
Playing the Playboy
Engaging the Boss
Stripping the Billionaire

Willow Park Series
Married for Christmas
A Baby for Easter
A Family for Christmas
Reconciled for Easter
Home for Christmas

One Night Novellas
One Night with her Best Friend
One Night in the Ice Storm

One Night with her Bodyguard
One Night with her Boss
One Night with her Roommate
One Night with the Best Man

The Protectors Series (co-written with Samantha Chase)
Protecting his Best Friend's Sister
Protecting the Enemy
Protecting the Girl Next Door
Protecting the Movie Star

Standalones
A Negotiated Marriage
Listed
Bittersweet
Missing
Revival
Holiday Heat
Salvation
Excavated
Overexposed
Road Tripping
Chasing Jane
Late Fall
Fooling Around
Married by Contract
Trophy Wife
Bay Song
Her Reluctant Billionaire
Second Best
CourtShip

Made in the USA
Columbia, SC
01 June 2019